Ice Cream Lover

Baldwin Village, Book 2

Jackie Lau

Copyright © 2019 Jackie Lau. All Rights Reserved.

First edition: May 2019
ISBN: 978-1-7753047-8-4

Editor: Latoya C. Smith, LCS Literary Services

Cover Design: Flirtation Designs

Cover photograph: Shutterstock

For Mom

One of the last things I ever told you was that I'd started writing my first novel. I wish you were here to see everything that has happened since. I miss you so much.

ONCE UPON A TIME, I loved ice cream.

But not anymore. Now the thought of ice cream on a hot summer's day makes me gag.

I know, I know, you're probably wondering what kind of monster hates ice cream.

It's not because I'm lactose intolerant, or because I don't have a sweet tooth. Seriously, don't keep me away from my chocolate, unless you want to get hurt. A guy at work stole a chocolate from the box I keep under my desk, and he's still scared of me after the murderous look I gave him.

It's not because I was run over by an ice cream truck as a child. I have good memories of the ice cream truck and the cheery music it played as it made its way through our neighborhood. My sister and I would beg my mother for a few coins so we could buy a chocolate-vanilla twist. She wouldn't usually give in, but occasionally, she did.

I have other good memories of ice cream, too. I remember going to the beach with my family, and there was a miraculous ice cream parlor nearby with fifty flavors. Fifty! It was paradise. Out of all those flavors, I chose one called "garbage." I may have been a little obsessed with garbage trucks at the time, plus it looked like it had *everything* in it. How exciting! Six-year-old me thought it was delicious.

On my very first date, when I was sixteen, I took the girl out for ice cream and we shared a banana split with chocolate ice cream and hot fudge sauce. And on my first date with Lisa, I took her to a little bakery in downtown Toronto that's famous for its ice cream sandwiches, made with freshly-baked cookies and gourmet ice cream.

Once, that was a nice memory. But now...

I look at the book in my lap, which has a close-up of an ice cream sandwich on the cover, and shudder.

It's a warm day in early May. I cleaned off my balcony earlier, and now I'm reclined on a lounge chair with this horrible book in my hands. It came out a year ago, and it promptly became a Globe and Mail bestseller before it started hitting the lists in the US. I've been avoiding it, but I feel like I ought to read the whole thing.

After all, it was written by Lisa Mathieson.

The woman who left me at the altar.

There I was, standing at the front of the church, sweating profusely in my tuxedo, four groomsmen next to me. Something was wrong. I could feel it. Shouldn't the ceremony have started already?

Then my sister, Adrienne, came hurrying down the aisle.

She was supposed to be the first bridesmaid to enter, but she was told to walk slowly and regally, stopping every now and then for the photographer to take a picture. Instead, she was running, her fancy updo askew.

Apparently, Lisa had just climbed out a window.

My fiancée might have left me without a word, but she did, ultimately, use lots of words to describe the experience. She wrote a self-help book slash memoir called *Embrace Your Inner Ice*

Cream Sandwich: How to Find the Positive You in a World of Negativity.

Guess who was the biggest source of negativity in her life?

Me.

I might not have read the whole book yet, but back when it came out, I read the reviews, as well as the chapter that's all about me. She renamed me Marvin Wong in the book but kept the other details the same.

Now, don't get me wrong. She didn't accuse me of mistreating her. No, she called me "a cross between Eeyore and Oscar the Grouch on steroids"—a slight exaggeration, in my opinion—who was a crappy boyfriend.

So, yeah, I got skewered in an international bestseller that encourages people to find their inner ice cream sandwiches.

Can you blame me for hating ice cream now?

I wonder how Lisa would describe *my* inner ice cream sandwich. Probably dry, tasteless cookies, filled with the dirty snow that lines the Toronto streets in the winter.

And seriously. Finding your inner ice cream sandwich?

What the hell is up with that bullshit?

Last I heard, Lisa had sold the film rights to the book, though I'm not sure how a self-help book slash memoir would be made into a movie. I assume I'd be one of the characters, though. On the plus side, given Hollywood's tendency to whitewash, I'd probably end up being played by some white dude named Chris, so it wouldn't really be me at all.

Or maybe they wouldn't whitewash me and I'd end up being played by another Chris: Chris Pang from *Crazy Rich Asians*.

I suppose that wouldn't be the end of the world.

After Lisa left me at the altar, she jetted off to Portugal and Spain, where she met some guy named Hernando or Fernando, who's apparently less of a grumpy bastard than I am.

I read the dedication in the book. *For Fernando, the love of my life.*

Oh, barf.

I'm about to start the first chapter when my phone rings. It's Adrienne. Usually it pisses me off when people call rather than text me—as Adrienne well knows—but now, I'm thankful for the disruption.

"How are you enjoying the weather?" she asks.

"I'm reading on the balcony with beer and chocolate."

"Sounds lovely."

I don't tell her what I'm reading. "What's up?"

"Nathan is going to Seattle on Monday. For a month."

Nathan, her husband, works for a software company that's setting up a Seattle office. The plan was that he'd fly out to make sure everything got up and running smoothly, but they keep changing the dates around on him.

"Is this for sure?" I ask.

"Yeah." She sighs. "A whole month. I was hoping it wouldn't happen until Mom and Dad were back from Hong Kong, so they could help with Michelle, but the timing stinks. I was wondering if you could watch her next Saturday?"

My sister is a pharmacist, and lately she's been working Saturday shifts, whereas I have a Monday to Friday job in finance. Michelle, her daughter, is five years old.

"Sure," I say, because my sister is in a bit of a bind, though I'm unsure of how Michelle and I will get along for a full day.

"Awesome. I'll bring her over to your place around seven thirty, and I'll pick her up by five. It'll be easier than you coming out here, plus there's a shop near your condo that Michelle wants to visit."

"What is it?"

"Well…" She hesitates. "It's an ice cream shop."

Given how much I hate ice cream, you'd think I might refuse.

But I'm not a child. I'm a thirty-two-year-old man with two university degrees. It's not like I can't stand to be in the same room as a bowl of ice cream. That would be truly pathetic.

No, I can do this. It might be uncomfortable and bring up some unpleasant associations, but if I can read Lisa's book, I can visit a stupid ice cream parlor with my niece, though I won't be getting any for myself.

However...

"The last time I took Michelle out for ice cream," I say, "it did not go well."

That was more than three years ago, only a few weeks before I was supposed to get married. I decided I could be the cool uncle who snuck her sweets.

Well, I'm her only uncle, so it's not like I was competing for the title of "cool uncle" with anyone. But when I heard the ice cream truck come down the street, I figured, why not?

I got a chocolate-vanilla twist for each of us, and she just stood there on the sidewalk, admiring the swirls, for a minute. Halfway through my own ice cream cone, I told her to hurry up because it was going to melt. So she took a bite...

...and promptly started crying, then threw it on the ground.

Let me be clear. She didn't start crying because she dropped her ice cream. The tears came first.

"It's disgusting!" she said between sobs.

You see, my niece is a food snob. We hadn't realized the full extent of it at the time, but now we know she has a better chance of enjoying blue cheese or Kalamata olives than pepperoni pizza. The foods most children love? Michelle won't touch them. Expensive stinky cheese? Probably going to be okay.

Fortunately, she doesn't cry and throw stuff on the ground quite as often now, but still.

"This will be different," Adrienne assures me. "Ginger Scoops is a fancy place that specializes in Asian flavors—green tea, Vietnamese coffee, lychee, things like that. Michelle is excited to go. She keeps talking about it. She saw it the last time we were downtown, and she was sad when I said we couldn't go in because she'd already had a treat that day."

"Fine, fine," I grumble.

"Thanks, Drew. You're the best."

I end the call and return to *Embrace Your Inner Ice Cream Sandwich*. Part 1 is titled "Before I Found My Ice Cream Sandwich." The first two chapters describe Lisa's childhood and university years in breezy language. She paints herself as an overachiever who was always listening to what other people wanted and never thought about what *she* wanted.

I laugh at parts that I'm sure were not meant to be funny. Here's the thing about Lisa: she wasn't lazy, but she was far from an overachiever, and it's a little hilarious that she sees her former self that way.

Then I get to the third chapter, which I read a year ago, but I re-read it now. "Chapter 3: Marvin Wong*." At the bottom of the page: "*Names have been changed to protect the innocent and not-so-innocent."

She describes me as a grumpy stick-in-the-mud who was always telling her "no." Who stifled her spirit and creative energy. She tells a story of how I refused to take a weeklong vacation to New England with her, but she doesn't mention that she asked at the last minute, and I couldn't get five days off work with only a week's notice. It's not like that was my fault, and I would have been happy to go some other time.

Am I heartbroken? Not anymore. Sure, Lisa was the woman I thought I'd marry, but that was years ago now. I'm over her.

I'm a little bitter, though. Most people don't have accounts of their failed relationships published in twenty-three languages and read by millions of people around the world. Everyone in my life knows; I can't hide from it.

And I can't help thinking that relationships just aren't worth it.

I was already thinking that after our wedding that didn't happen, but having it appear in a bestselling book was just icing on the wedding cake...that no one ended up eating.

I haven't been on a date since I was left at the altar. When I heard my ex had written a book called *Embrace Your Inner Ice Cream Sandwich*, I burst into laughter, and as it raced up the charts, ice cream lost its appeal.

I didn't set out to hate ice cream. Honestly, I didn't. A few weeks after the book hit the top spot on the Globe and Mail bestseller list, I bought some dark chocolate ice cream—the good stuff—and served myself a small bowl.

And promptly felt sick.

The next day, I tried again. Same response.

I haven't eaten ice cream since.

Once upon a time, I might have enjoyed a scoop of chocolate ice cream on a day like today, the first nice day of the year. I may have even enjoyed it with a pretty woman by my side.

Instead, I'm alone with a bourbon barrel-aged imperial stout and a book with a ginormous ice cream sandwich on the cover. My mouth twisting in a rueful grin, I raise my bottle of beer.

"Cheers," I say, to no one but me.

IT's 11:59. Finally. I've been anxiously awaiting noon for the past hour.

I walk to the front door of Ginger Scoops and flip the sign from "closed" to "open." It's the first Sunday in May, and it's unseasonably hot, like yesterday. Should be good for business.

Before I head behind the counter, I read over the list of ice cream flavors on the blackboard hanging from the wall. Black sesame...yes. Ginger...yes. But I have a feeling I'm missing something.

The strawberry-lychee sorbet! How could I have forgotten? I recently perfected it, and this will be the first time it's available for purchase.

"Everything okay, Chloe?" Valerie asks.

"Yep!" I hide my anxiety behind a cheerful smile. "Just adding strawberry-lychee sorbet to the list."

I set down the piece of chalk, then straighten all the tables and chairs one more time.

Valerie shakes her head. "You've already done that half a dozen times. They're fine."

I know, but I can't help it. I return behind the counter with a sigh.

Ginger Scoops is my baby. My very own ice cream shop. It's been open for a month now, and I need to prove to my father that it wasn't a colossal mistake. That I can do this.

I glance at the framed photo on the wall near the counter. It's a picture of me and my mother at an ice cream parlor in The Beaches. I'm five, holding a strawberry ice cream cone, and we're smiling at each other.

I turn back to Valerie Chow. We've been friends for a long time, and she's working for me while she figures out what to do with her life. If business is good, maybe I'll also hire a high school student for weekends in the summer.

I hope business is good enough for that.

It's 12:03, and nobody has come in yet. I tell myself it's okay.

"Here." Valerie shoves a cup of tea in my face. "Stop freaking out. It's going to be fine."

Easy for her to say. She doesn't have all of her money invested in this. She hasn't borrowed money from her father, her aunt, and the bank.

The chimes on the door tinkle. A mother and her daughter—perhaps four years old—walk in.

"Can you hold me up so I can see?" the girl asks her mother.

"Sure, sweetie." The mom picks her up, and she looks at the tubs of ice cream.

"I want the purple one, please!"

The mom turns to me. "What is it?"

"Taro," I say.

"Perhaps she could try a bite first?"

I scoop up a tiny amount of taro ice cream on a plastic spoon and hand it to the girl. Her eyes light up. "Yes, that one!"

I smile as I scoop taro ice cream into a cone for her, and her mother asks for matcha cheesecake ice cream. They sit at a table by the window, and something tugs at my heart as I see them together. I glance back at the picture on the wall.

But then a large group enters, and I am blessedly too busy to think about my mother anymore.

∾

At two o'clock, there's a lull in business, and I debate what to have for lunch. I usually bring food with me, but I didn't get a chance to pack anything this morning.

Hmm. I could go to Pupusa Hut or Hogtown Poke, or I could visit Sarah at Happy As Pie and have a pulled pork pie. So many choices.

I've always loved this section of Baldwin between Beverley and McCaul, just east of Chinatown, where the old homes have been turned into restaurants and cafes and other business. When I saw that this unit was available, I jumped at the chance, even though the rent was a little more than I'd wanted to pay.

I'm about to leave to get a couple of pupusas when my father walks in.

"Dad!" I say. "I'm so glad you came."

I'd hoped he would come for opening day last month, but he didn't.

At least he's here now.

He looks around, confusion on his face, as though he doesn't know how he managed to find himself in an ice cream shop.

"You decided to paint the back wall pink," he says.

"I did." It's a deep raspberry pink, and I think it's pretty and cheerful.

Dad doesn't seem to approve, just like he didn't approve of me opening an ice cream shop rather than finishing university and applying to dental school.

Everyone loves ice cream, but most people dread going to the dentist. As a child, however, I didn't mind the dentist at all. The hygienist was super nice and praised my brushing skills, the dentist always made me a balloon animal, and the receptionist gave me a pack of stickers—usually the scratch-and-sniff kind—after each appointment.

I decided I wanted to be a dentist when I was seven or eight, and I didn't waver from that plan for over a decade. I studied life sciences in university.

But I never graduated, and I never got around to taking the DAT.

There's a before and an after in my life. After my mom was killed in a car accident, everything changed. I quit university in the middle of the term, and I've never wanted to go back. Dad was supportive of me taking a break, but after a year went by and I showed no interest in returning, he got frustrated. Still, he gave me some money to start the ice cream shop. I'm pretty sure he thinks that after a few months of running my own business, I'll see it's a foolish endeavor and decide to go back to school.

That's not going to happen, though.

Once upon a time, I wanted to prevent cavities, but now, I want to give people cavities.

Well, no. I don't actually want people to get cavities; I just want to give them something sweet and satisfying, something that makes them happy.

"Which flavors would you like?" I ask my father.

"Green tea and ginger," he says.

"How about I put them in a bubble waffle for you?" I point to a plastic frame on the counter, which has a picture of a waffle with large bubbles—sort of like bubble wrap—that's rolled into a cone and contains two scoops of ice cream. "They're popular in Hong Kong."

He nods.

I pour the batter into the waffle maker, and my father glances at the photo of my mom and me on the wall. He doesn't say anything.

When the waffle is finished and filled with ice cream, I tell Valerie that I'm going to the patio with my father for a few minutes. We head out the door and take a seat on a bench under a pink umbrella.

"What do you think?" I ask my dad after he tries a bite of the green tea ice cream.

"I'm not sure how I feel about tea-flavored ice cream." He leans forward. "This is what I don't understand about your business. The green tea ice cream, the red bean-coconut ice cream, the waffles from Hong Kong…"

"It's an Asian ice cream shop."

"I know. But why?"

I stiffen. "Why not?"

You're not Asian, I imagine him thinking, but he doesn't say that out loud.

My white father thinks it's best to ignore race, to pretend it doesn't exist. He told me last year that he never thought of my Chinese-Canadian mother as being Chinese at all. But her experiences were different from his because of her family history and how she looked. It feels like he can't acknowledge that.

I don't think he truly understands that I'm biracial. He sees me as one of his own, as white, even though many of my facial features are in between his and my mother's, and I inherited her eye color and complexion.

I'm thankful for the latter. My father turns pink if he gets even a small amount of sun, and he walks around in an ugly, floppy brown hat for half the year—like now. I find the hat rather endearing, though. Very *Dad*. Since my mother is dead and I don't have any siblings, he's my only surviving close relative.

I would do anything to make him happy, except the one thing he wants me to do.

"The ginger is really good," he says. "Yes, I quite like that one."

"I'll give you some other samples to try afterward." I should have done that earlier.

"How much ice cream do you eat, now that you own an ice cream shop?"

"Not every day, but more than I should, probably."

He proceeds to give me a lecture on nutrition, telling me that I need to make sure I get enough vegetables and protein.

I don't mind these lectures, the ones that aren't about my career. I like being reminded that I still have someone to parent me, even though I'm twenty-five.

We go back inside, and he tries the strawberry-lychee sorbet, the taro ice cream, and the red bean-coconut ice cream. He likes the first two, but not the red bean one, which doesn't surprise me. He never liked red bean mooncakes, which my mother always bought for the Mid-Autumn Festival.

Dad reminds me of my grandmother's eightieth birthday party next Sunday, then gives me a hug.

"Love you," he says.

"I love you, too, Dad."

You never know when it'll be your last chance to say those words.

They're the opposite of what I said to my mother the last time I saw her alive.

We close at six o'clock, and I look at the sales numbers after Valerie goes home. They're not bad, but not great. Ginger Scoops will need to do better than this on hot summer weekends if it's going to succeed.

And it *has* to succeed. I've put so much into this. All the money I saved from my various jobs. Money from my family. I took a couple courses to help me learn how to run a business.

Until a few months ago, I lived with my father to minimize my expenses, despite the awkwardness between us.

But most importantly, I did this in memory of my mother. I know that seems like a frivolous way to honor my mother, but it feels right.

For that reason, more than anything, I have to make this work.

[3]
DREW

"It's so pretty, Uncle Drew!" Michelle says. "Take a picture, please."

Dutifully, I take out my phone and snap a picture of our salmon poke bowl. In addition to salmon, it has avocado, nori, edamame beans, and some kind of sauce in a zig-zag pattern, all on top of rice. Since the bowls are too big for Michelle to have her own, we ordered one to share, and now I put her portion in an empty bowl.

We're sitting in Hogtown Poke on Baldwin Street, and I am, unfortunately, soaking wet. It was supposed to be nice weather today, but instead, the sky decided to take a piss on us, and then Michelle jumped in an enormous puddle in her sparkly purple rain boots, leaving my pants soaked. I can't wait to go home and change into some dry clothes, but first, I have to finish my poke bowl and take my niece out for ice cream.

Michelle has a bite and chews thoughtfully.

"What do you think?" I ask.

"It's good," she says, "but you know what would make it better? Wakame salad."

"They have it as a topping for some of the other bowls. Let me see if I can get you some."

I head to the counter and return a minute later with a small serving of wakame salad. Michelle dumps it in her bowl and takes a bite.

"Perfect," she says.

Most five-year-olds wouldn't say that about seaweed salad, but Michelle is not a normal kid when it comes to food.

She didn't get it from her mother, that's for sure. Adrienne is the exact opposite of a food snob, and she's the world's most useless cook. She's the kind of person who'd eat a bag of potato chips for dinner. My niece, however, is already pretty good at cooking, and I fully expect her to win some kind of Mini Iron Chef competition by the time she's ten.

We eat in silence, and when we're finished, we head out into the pouring rain. Fortunately, Ginger Scoops is right across the street.

Unfortunately, it looks like a unicorn threw up inside the ice cream shop.

One wall is solid pink. The chairs and tables are white and pastel green, and there are fairy lights strung across the walls. In one corner sits a rocking horse, a rainbow painted on the wall above it.

Oh, boy. Who would decorate a business like this?

I jolt back when I see the woman behind the counter. She has dark brown hair and eyes, and I think she might be biracial like Michelle. She's wearing a fussy apron with ruffles, and okay, I'll admit, she's very pretty, and that's probably why I jolted back in surprise. She's smiling, so I try to smile back at her, though I probably end up looking like Shrek.

"Read me the flavors, Uncle Drew!" Michelle says.

I read her the list and ask what she wants.

"I don't know. They all sound good."

"You can try them first." The woman is still smiling.

Michelle is super excited. "Okay, I'd like to try the green tea-strawberry, the passionfruit, the black sesame, the matcha cheesecake—"

"That's too many," I say.

"It's no problem," says the woman behind the counter. "It's not busy." She scoops out a small amount of pink ice cream and hands it to me over the counter. I give it to Michelle.

My niece tries the ice cream and thinks for a moment. "It's good, but it could use a little more green tea."

The woman cocks her head to the side. "Yes, I agree. I plan to make some minor changes for the next batch."

"You make it yourself?" Michelle asks.

"I do."

"That's so cool."

The woman hands me another spoon, this one with yellow ice cream—presumably the passionfruit—and our fingers brush. It feels like I'm being zapped with the rainbows and stardust flowing through her veins.

After Michelle has tried all four flavors, she orders passion-fruit and matcha cheesecake.

"Wait a second," I say, playing the role of responsible adult. "You're not getting a double scoop. You can have the smallest size."

"But Uncle Drew—"

"She can have two flavors in a kiddie size." The woman starts to scoop out the matcha cheesecake, then looks up at me. "What would you like?"

I observe a coffeepot. Thank God. "One coffee. No cream, no sugar."

"You're not having ice cream?" Michelle asks, horrified.

"You know I don't like ice cream."

"I thought you were joking! How can you not like ice cream? It's good ice cream, not like that ice cream truck you took me to when I was little."

I'm surprised she remembers that, since she wasn't even three.

I'm also surprised that the lady behind the counter doesn't expire in horror when I say I don't like ice cream. Instead, she goes into business mode.

"If you're lactose intolerant," she says, "the ginger-lime sorbet and the strawberry-lychee sorbet are dairy free."

"I'm not lactose intolerant."

"If you usually find ice cream too sweet, the ginger-lime sorbet—"

"I have no problem with sugar."

"Oh. I figured, since you asked for your coffee without sugar…"

"I like my coffee black, that's all. I just don't like ice cream."

She shakes her head. "I don't understand people like you."

And frankly, I don't understand people who wear ruffled aprons and work in ice cream shops that look like My Little Pony.

"If you like coffee," she says, "are you sure I can't tempt you with Vietnamese coffee ice cream?"

"Very sure."

"Is the problem that you don't like cold things? Does it give you a headache? I could microwave it for you."

"Then it wouldn't really be ice cream anymore, would it?"

"I wouldn't have to melt it. I could make it the consistency of pudding, maybe?"

"No."

Although I'm the freak who drinks beer at room temperature —imperial stouts, in my opinion, have more flavor when they're not ice cold—I'm not eating microwaved ice cream.

No, not happening.

"Chocolate-raspberry?" she suggests.

"No."

"Taro? It's nice and…purple-y."

She's so earnest. It's kind of cute.

I hold back a laugh. "No, thank you."

"The matcha cheesecake ice cream is really quite excellent, trust me."

"If it was an actual cheesecake, not in ice cream form, I would eat it." I like the matcha cheesecake at the Japanese cheesecake place near where I live. "But as I said, I just don't like ice cream."

She peers at me as though trying to determine whether I'm a serial killer.

"Fine," she says with a sigh. "One black coffee, nothing else." After handing Michelle her cup of ice cream, she pours my coffee. She looks a bit deflated, and I consider ordering a small cup of ice cream just to see her smile again.

What the hell?

Nope, no way is that happening.

Why did that thought even occur to me?

I wonder if this woman has read *Embrace Your Inner Ice Cream Sandwich*. She probably doesn't need that book, though. I suspect she's already hopped up on sprinkles and positivity and knows exactly what her inner ice cream sandwich is.

There are no ice cream sandwiches on the menu here, however.

"Anything else you'd like?" she asks.

"No, that'll be all, thank you."

I pay for our order, then Michelle and I sit down at a table near the window. She looks very pleased with her cup, and she proceeds to eat in silence. She usually eats quietly, as though the wheels in her head are spinning, analyzing all the flavors.

"I love this place," she says when she finishes.

"I'm glad," I say. "Why don't we stay here a little longer, until the rain lets up?"

"Can I have more ice cream, please?"

I give her a look. "You know you're only allowed one treat. Why don't you try the rocking pony?"

"It's not a pony. It's a unicorn! Don't you see its horn?"

"The rocking unicorn. Right. I misspoke."

Michelle climbs onto the unicorn, and I sip my coffee.

Okay, I admit maybe I wanted to stay a bit longer because I wanted to take another look at the woman behind the counter. Right now, she's reaching for something on a high shelf, and I can't help admiring the great view of her ass. I'm about to ask if she needs help, but nope, she's got it.

Once upon a time, I might have asked her out. But not now. I've already been left at the altar once; I've already inspired one journey of self-discovery that led to a bestselling book. I don't need to do it again.

Of course, I could try to change who I am as a person, but the two days I spent attempting to be cheerful and charming last fall were a disaster. Everyone looked at me funny, probably thinking I was on drugs, and it felt so forced and uncomfortable.

No, I am who I am, and I have exactly what I want out of life right now.

At least, that's what I keep telling myself.

"Come on, time to go," I say to Michelle.

"Take a picture of me riding the unicorn first!"

I pull out my phone again and snap the requested photo. Then I take my little niece's hand and lead her out into the rain. I swear I can feel the eyes of the woman behind the counter on me as we leave.

But that's probably just my imagination.

[4]
CHLOE

It's too bad about the permanent scowl on his face. Otherwise, the East Asian man who just walked out the door with his niece would be incredibly handsome. At one point he attempted to smile, and he looked like a demented puppet.

It's too bad about the scowl and his attitude toward ice cream.

Honestly, what kind of person hates ice cream?

Not that it matters. I'll probably never see him again.

The chimes above the door tinkle, and Valerie walks in, along with Sarah Winters. Sarah owns Happy As Pie across the street, which makes both sweet and savory pies. Ice cream has always been my dessert of choice, but her strawberry-rhubarb pie is to die for, as is her berry crumble pie and her lemon-lime tart and her butter tarts…

Okay, I just really like Sarah's pies.

The savory ones are good, too. Valerie sits down at a table and opens a box with a steaming braised lamb and rosemary pie—I can tell by the smell—and I groan.

"Don't worry, there's some for you, too." She sets down another box.

Sarah and I join her at the table. There's no one else here right now, and it's pouring rain outside, so I can take a break. I moan as I put the first bite of pie into my mouth. The filling is rich and delicious, surrounded by a flaky crust.

"How's business today?" I ask.

"Slow." Sarah sighs.

"Same here."

Valerie stuffs another bite into her mouth. "What about the hot dad I just saw walking out the door?"

I give her a look. "For starters, that was his niece, not his daughter." Though of course that doesn't mean he couldn't also have children of his own, but "Uncle Drew" was what the little girl called him. "Second of all, he ordered a black coffee and refused to try any ice cream. Says he hates it."

Sarah and Valerie let out faux gasps, as though I said he was the devil.

"With that attitude," I say, "I bet he has little success with women. Or men."

"Perhaps he's a very nice person other than his hatred for ice cream," Sarah says.

"If he hates ice cream, he probably hates lots of other lovely things, too. Like puppies and rainbows and gingersnaps and"—I look at Sarah—"your decadent chocolate tart."

She gasps again. "No. He couldn't!"

I point at the box in her hands. "God, I hope there's some chocolate tart in there."

Sarah opens it up. There is indeed a slice of chocolate tart, as well as slices of spiced apple pie and strawberry-rhubarb pie. "You know how we talked about having pie à la mode specials? Let's try a few things now."

"Yes!" Admittedly, part of the reason I want to do these specials is for the taste testing.

It's amazing to have a friend who owns a pie shop that is literally across the street. Happy As Pie has been open for a year or so, and Valerie and I got to know Sarah when we'd pop in for coffee—and sometimes pie, of course—in the months when we were setting up Ginger Scoops. A couple months ago, she started dating Josh Yu, who hired her to cater his Pi Day party.

"Let's try the spiced apple first." I put the slice of pie on a plate, then go behind the counter and survey the tubs of ice cream. Ginger?

Yes, definitely ginger.

I add a generous scoop to the plate and grab three forks, then return to the table. The apple pie is still warm, and oh my God, this is an amazing combination.

Next, we try the chocolate tart with a few different ice creams: Vietnamese coffee, passionfruit, and green tea.

"I like it best with the Vietnamese coffee," I say.

"I agree," Sarah says. "Although it's good with the passionfruit, too. I've always been a fan of chocolate and fruit combos and— Valerie! Did you just finish the Vietnamese coffee? I was going to have more."

Valerie looks…not at all guilty.

We eat the strawberry-rhubarb pie with vanilla ice cream and decide we'll have our first pie à la mode special next weekend. Sarah will give me a pie, I'll give her some ice cream, and we'll both sell the special.

Pie and ice cream and friends on a rainy afternoon. Not a bad way to pass the time.

The ice cream-hating customer pops into my mind again, and I push him right back out.

I have better things to think about.

I clutch my drink and survey the backyard. It's five thirty, and normally I'd be at Ginger Scoops at this time on a Sunday, but Valerie is closing up by herself today so I can attend my paternal grandmother's eightieth birthday party.

My father has a large family. He's one of six kids, and all of them had children. Many of my cousins are married, and a couple have started having babies.

It's a big contrast to my mother's family. My mom only had one sibling—my Aunt Anita—and she doesn't have kids. So I was the only grandchild on my mom's side, whereas on my father's side, I'm one of fourteen.

It should have been lots of fun to have so many cousins close to my age, and at times it was, but I always felt a bit separate from them. All of my father's siblings' spouses are white; my mother and I stood out. Now that my mother's gone, it's just me.

My grandparents were always polite, though a little distant, with my mother. They didn't voice any disapproval over my parents' marriage—not to my knowledge, anyway—but there was something different in how they interacted with my mother in comparison with their other sons- and daughters-in-law. Me, they treated like their other grandchildren, more or less.

Sometimes I get annoyed with myself for feeling like I don't belong. They're not just my dad's family; they're my family, too, even if they don't look quite like me.

I assume it's normal to feel like you don't fit in anywhere when you're biracial. You're both, and yet you're neither. But shouldn't I at least feel like I belong with my own family?

I have no Chinese family in Toronto. My maternal grandparents are dead, and Aunt Anita lives in New York City and hasn't visited in years. With only white relatives here, I feel like my Chinese heritage is slipping away from me, and I've had an identity crisis of sorts since my mother's death.

But how much connection did I have to my Chinese heritage before? I don't speak the language. In the absence of that, there's the food, but I can't cook much of the traditional fare I remember my Chinese grandmother making so many years ago.

All I have is the shape of my facial features to suggest that I'm not quite white.

A few years ago, I tried reading books about Chinese history and learning Mandarin, but it didn't give me what I was looking for. My mother had never been to China, and my family didn't speak Mandarin. They spoke Toisanese, but there are no Toisanese classes in Toronto.

I push those thoughts out of my mind and take another sip of my drink as I look around the backyard. My grandparents bought this large house in Forest Hill many years ago, and it must be worth a fortune now. My grandfather passed away a few years ago, and my grandmother lives here alone. Although it's her birthday and she shouldn't have to cook, she insisted on supplying half the food. Right now she's putting out a "salad" with lime Jell-O, pineapple, whipped cream, and cream cheese. I loved that stuff as a child but don't particularly like it anymore; I eat it just for the nostalgia factor.

My cousin Lillian walks toward me. She's the cousin who's closest in age to me—she's ten months older—so we spent lots of time together as kids, but I haven't seen her in a while. She got married a year ago, and I notice her stomach is curving outward just a bit. Maybe she's pregnant...or maybe she's not, and it would be horribly awkward if I ask.

Knowing Lillian, she'll say something within the next thirty seconds anyway.

She envelops me in a hug. "It's so good to see you!"

"You, too. How's married life?"

"Great." She pats her belly. "We're expecting."

I hug her again, and we talk a little about her pregnancy and how she's started craving lime Jell-O salad.

"I actually made some last week," she says, and we laugh. "Terry wouldn't touch it."

"I just saw Grandma putting it out."

"Excellent. Before I forget…" She pulls her phone out of her purse and shows me a picture of a clean-cut blond dude. "What do you think?"

"Um, he's handsome?" I think that's the response she expects, though why, I'm not sure.

And although he's handsome, his smile doesn't do as much for me as Drew's scowl.

Hmph.

"Can I set you two up?" she asks.

"What?"

I wasn't expecting that, but perhaps I should have.

"I don't know why, but I have a feeling you'd be perfect for each other," Lillian says. "His name is Cody, and he's an engineer. One of Terry's friends."

I have a feeling my happily-married cousin is going to keep trying to set me up.

"I'm not interested in dating," I say. "Sorry. I'm trying to get the ice cream shop off the ground, and I don't have time."

"We were going to pop by yesterday, but then there was all that rain… Soon, I promise. I saw your pictures on Facebook—it looks amazing! But back to your love life. You can't just swear off men completely." She pauses. "Men or women, I mean."

In addition to being the only non-white person in my dad's family, I'm also the only one—to my knowledge—who isn't straight.

I shrug. "It's not a priority right now."

"What if Catherine Zeta-Jones divorced Michael Douglas and moved to Toronto and came into your ice cream shop one day?"

"Leave Catherine Zeta-Jones out of this!" Though, oh my God, it would be super cool if she came to Ginger Scoops.

"Fine. What if cartoon fox Robin Hood came to life and was a human but somehow still a fox at the same time—"

"Like, he was a fox shifter?"

"Yes! A fox shifter. Exactly."

Lillian and I used to watch the Disney movie all the time when we were kids.

"Alright," I say. "If cartoon fox Robin Hood comes to life, or if

Catherine Zeta-Jones divorces Michael Douglas and moves to Toronto, I will consider dating. Until then, no."

Being busy with Ginger Scoops is the reason I give everyone for why I'm not interested in relationships, even though it's not really true. Yes, I'm busy, but having some work-life balance is important—as I told Sarah when she was having doubts about dating Josh.

Up until this year, I actually did a fair bit of dating. Mostly men, occasionally women. Different races, different ages. But I couldn't quite connect with anyone. I feel like I don't belong when I'm with my family, and that's also how I've felt on every date I've gone on since my mom died. I even had a boyfriend for four months last year. I kept seeing him because he really liked me and he was such a sweet guy, but I still felt an uncomfortable distance with him. I kept thinking that would go away soon, but it never did, so I ended it.

It's like something is preventing me from truly feeling close to anyone. It used to be easy for me to feel a real connection with someone, but ever since my mom's death, it's been different.

Will I always be this way?

I hope not. Maybe in a few years, I'll try dating again, but for now, I'm not going to worry about it. I won't bother going on dates.

Not with clean-cut Cody, or any other person Lillian wants to set me up with.

Not with Drew.

Why on earth am I thinking about Drew? He's just a guy who came into my shop yesterday, nothing more.

I can't seem to get him out of my mind, though. His niece, too. She looks so much like me when I was younger that it's almost uncanny. I feel an odd surge of affection for this girl I don't know at all, just because she probably has the same background as me.

A bony hand touches my shoulder.

"Chloe!" Grandma says. "Here, have a deviled egg."

I take one off the tray. "It's your birthday. You shouldn't be walking around and serving food."

"What else am I going to do? Sit on a throne draped in red velvet and stroke my cat while one grandchild feeds me grapes and another rubs my feet?"

Lillian and I stare at her.

"You've given this a lot of thought," I say.

She laughs. "Your father was telling me about your ice cream shop the other day. He says you have green tea ice cream. Where did you get that idea?"

"It wasn't my idea. Lots of places serve it."

"I'll have to try it one day. I'll get John to take me there."

I know what will happen when my grandmother tries green tea ice cream. She'll say, "Well, that's interesting," and she'll smile...but she won't like it. It'll be too weird for her, and she'll go back to her meatloaf and deviled eggs and "normal" ice cream flavors like chocolate and butterscotch. Still, I'll be happy to see her at Ginger Scoops.

"And you." Grandma turns to Lillian. "Is pregnancy agreeing with you?"

Lillian smiles. "It's going fine."

"Maybe you'll be like me and do it six times."

"Somehow, I don't think that's going to happen."

"It's too expensive to raise six kids these days," Grandma says, "but look at the large family I have to celebrate my birthday." She sweeps one arm around the yard.

Most of us are here, though I haven't seen my dad yet, which is odd. He's usually early.

Just as I think that, he comes around the side of the house, wearing his ugly brown hat. He approaches us and kisses his mother on the cheek. "Happy birthday, Mom. And happy Mother's Day."

I stiffen. How did I forget that today is Mother's Day? It's usually hard to forget, what with all the ads telling you to make it a special day for your mother. The flowers, the cards. I guess I've been so pre-occupied with Ginger Scoops that I managed to push it out of my mind.

Now I feel a little guilty for not going to the cemetery.

Because that's what Mother's Day is now. Go-to-the-cemetery day.

Dad looks my way. He nods and gives me a small smile, and there's a sadness in his eyes that has become familiar in the past five years.

"Well," he says. "Shall I start the barbecue?"

When I get home that evening, I'm stuffed with burgers and pasta salad and cake. I'd been expecting a cheap vanilla sheet cake, but instead, my aunt bought three cakes from an expensive bakery, and God, they were good. The red velvet was my favorite. I pretended that I needed to try all three as research for ice cream flavors.

At least, that's what I told Lillian, and then I laughed at my own joke—I was desperate for laughter.

What I wouldn't give to be able to celebrate Mother's Day again.

MICHELLE'S EYES light up when she sees all the pies in the display case. I figured we'd have lunch on Baldwin Street again, then go to Ginger Scoops, and she decided on the pie shop. Personally, I was more intrigued by the Indonesian restaurant (Paulie's Laksa) and the Korean-Polish restaurant (K-Polish).

The Korean-Polish restaurant has a Korean section of the menu with bibimbap and stuff like that, then a Polish section, and lastly, a fusion section. The fusion menu has things like kimchi jjigae served in a potato pancake, and bulgogi pierogis. I'm not sure how good it would be, but I'm curious.

Michelle, however, is all about the pie.

"What's this one?" she asks the lady behind the counter.

"Pulled pork pie."

"And this one?"

"Braised lamb and rosemary."

"Let me read them for you," I say to Michelle, not wanting her to annoy the poor lady.

In addition to the four types of savory pie, which are all single-serving size, there are six sweet pies and tarts. There's also a special written on a little chalkboard on the counter. *Special of the day: Chocolate tart with Vietnamese coffee ice cream.*

Chocolate and coffee? You can't go wrong with those. I'm practically salivating.

And then I register what the sign actually says.

Vietnamese coffee *ice cream.*

I recoil as if I've been hit.

"…one slice of lemon-lime tart, and one slice of—"

"Hold on a second," I interrupt. "Michelle, are you ordering without me?"

"Yep! We're having pulled pork pie, chicken pot pie, braised lamb and rosemary pie, lemon-lime tart, pecan pie, and strawberry-rhubarb pie."

Michelle is not shy about ordering food at restaurants. She's also got an excellent memory. Whenever I read her a menu, she remembers every item.

"Were you trying to get some extra dessert past me?" I put my hands on my hips. "We're having dessert at Ginger Scoops, not here."

"But you're not having dessert at Ginger Scoops because you hate ice cream," my niece points out. "I ordered the lemon-lime tart, pecan pie, and strawberry-rhubarb pie for you."

"Yes, because what I need is three slices of pie."

"You're lots bigger than me, so you need lots more dessert."

"Let me guess," I say. "You were planning on trying all of these desserts?"

She nods vigorously. "But just a little bite."

"Uh-huh. I think you were planning on eating a lot more than a little bite, and it's not happening."

"But Uncle Drew…"

I turn to the lady behind the counter. "Sorry about that. We will have the pulled pork pie, the braised lamb and rosemary pie, and the lemon-lime tart."

The pulled pork pie is delicious, and the rosemary lamb pie is pretty damn good, too.

"When Daddy comes back from Seattle," Michelle says, "I'm going to ask him to make pie with me. Do you think it's difficult?"

"I don't know. I've never baked pie before."

I have another bite of the pulled pork pie and look at the ice cream shop across the street. I wonder if the same woman will be there again today.

We finish the savory pies, then start on the lemon-lime tart. Even though Michelle's getting ice cream afterward, I let her have half of it. I'm her uncle. I'm allowed to spoil her a little if I want to.

Mm. That really is some quality tart.

When we're finished, we head across to Ginger Scoops. Michelle skips excitedly through the door, just like my stupid heart.

The woman is here again today. There's no one else at the counter, but a few people are sitting on the patio, enjoying their ice cream.

"You're back," she says.

"I am." I try to sound suitably grumpy, even though part of me is glad to be here.

"I'm surprised to see you, given you proclaimed your hatred of ice cream last time."

She's wearing the same apron again today, a simple black T-shirt underneath.

She's just as beautiful as I remember.

"It's not my choice," I say. "My niece really likes it here, so"—I shrug—"here we are."

"Perhaps I can tempt you with our special?" The woman points to the bottom of the blackboard that lists the ice cream flavors. "Chocolate tart with Vietnamese coffee ice cream."

Wait...what?

"We were just at Happy As Pie," I say, "and they had exactly the same special."

"I know. It's a collaboration. What do you think? I'll be sure to give you only a small serving of ice cream."

"No, thank you."

"You don't think chocolate tart with coffee ice cream sounds delicious?"

"I like chocolate—"

"OMG, call the press! He actually likes chocolate!"

I hide a smile. "But as I said, I don't like ice cream."

"How about spiced apple pie with ginger ice cream? Or strawberry-rhubarb pie with vanilla ice cream? Do those sound good? Or maybe—"

"What part of 'I don't like ice cream' do you not understand?"

"Fine." Her lips thin. "Just a plain black coffee?"

"That's right."

She turns to Michelle and gives her a wide smile that she didn't give me. "What would you like to try today? Do you want me to read off the flavors for you?"

"I want to try the Vietnamese coffee," Michelle says.

The woman looks doubtful that my young niece will like coffee-flavored ice cream but gives her a sample anyway. Me, on the other hand? I'm afraid Michelle will enjoy it and order a scoop. How much caffeine does the ice cream have? Will she be bouncing off the wall from a combined sugar and caffeine high?

To my relief, Michelle scrunches up her nose. "Ew. Why do adults like this stuff?"

She tries a few more flavors and settles on chocolate-raspberry and ginger. We take a seat at a table inside, me with my coffee and her with her ice cream.

"Do you know what next weekend is?" she asks.

"No, what is it?"

"My birthday!"

Right. I don't know how I forgot about that. "Are you having a party?"

"Of course I'm having a party! Are you coming?"

"I wasn't invited. Is it a party just for your friends?"

"You can come, too," she says.

"How generous of you." I wonder what her birthday party will entail. Presumably the food will be good, because Michelle will not stand for anything else. Will they play pin-the-tail-on-the-donkey? Will they whack at a piñata? Will ten girls in party dresses and pigtails run around screaming for two hours and throw Shopkins at each other while they demolish a charcuterie board?

We lapse into silence. I look out the window as I sip my coffee, and when I turn my gaze back to Michelle, she's staring at the woman behind the counter.

I don't blame her. The woman in question is very pretty, but...

"It's not polite to stare at people," I whisper.

Michelle doesn't listen. "She looks like me, don't you think? Will I be as pretty as her when I grow up?"

"Of course you will. But please stop staring."

"I've never seen someone who looks so much like me before. Are we related?"

"I hope not."

I'm certainly having thoughts about this woman that would be inappropriate if we were related. For example, I'm currently picturing her with nothing under that apron.

But at the same time, my heart squeezes, because I know—sort of—what it's like to be Michelle. When I was her age, there were very few books at the library about kids who looked like me. I had family and friends who looked like me, but books and movies were a different matter.

Michelle, however, doesn't know anyone who looks quite like her. She's biracial, and her features are a mix of her parents'; she doesn't strongly favor either one.

She goes up to the counter. "What's your name?"

"Chloe," says the lady.

Chloe. I file this away for future use.

"I'm Michelle. We look like sisters, don't we? I always wanted a sister, but even though I ask for one every birthday, I haven't gotten one yet."

"We do! I looked so much like you when I was your age."

"Do you have a sister?"

Chloe shakes her head before leading my niece back to the table.

After Michelle finishes her ice cream and I finish my coffee, I take her hand and give Chloe a curt nod.

"What would you like to do now?" I ask my niece.

"I want to draw!"

As it turns out, Michelle wants to draw ice cream cones. Back at my apartment, she fills four pieces of paper with pictures of ice cream in a variety of colors. She asks me how to spell "chocolate" and "green tea" and "ginger" so she can label each one.

By the time Adrienne shows up at five thirty, Michelle has moved on to drawing a fruit and vegetable garden. However, she seems to think everything grows on trees. Not only are there apple and pear trees, but also carrot and tomato trees.

Perhaps a trip to the farm would be educational.

"Mommy!" Michelle runs over and gives Adrienne a hug.

"Did you have a good day, honey? Did you behave for Uncle Drew?"

She nods, and Adrienne raises an eyebrow at me.

"I invited Uncle Drew to my birthday party," Michelle says. "Is that okay?"

Adrienne turns to me. "I was going to ask you to help, actually, if you're free next Saturday. Nathan isn't around, and I'd like to have a second adult there."

"Sure," I say, even though supervising a children's birthday party sounds like the opposite of fun.

"In fact…" Adrienne leads me to the balcony door and drops her voice. "Michelle really likes that ice cream shop. She talked about it all week. Do you think you could pick up some ice cream from there for the party?"

Well, isn't this just great. I'm going to have to pay an extra visit to the ice cream shop that looks like a unicorn palace and see Chloe again.

My pulse beats quicker at the thought.

Calm the fuck down, I tell my body.

"Yeah, sure," I say. "What flavors should I get?"

"Why don't you try all the flavors and pick the ones you like best?"

I look at my sister in horror.

"Just kidding." She laughs. "Whatever Michelle likes. Something that would complement the chocolate ganache cake I'm picking up on Saturday morning."

Once Adrienne and Michelle leave, I grab a beer and a half-finished bar of dark chocolate, then head to the balcony with *Embrace Your Inner Ice Cream Sandwich.*

I'm more than halfway through the book. The part I'm on now is about how to identify your inner ice cream sandwich. Lisa describes her own inner ice cream sandwich as oatmeal-raisin cookies with a scoop of mocha ice cream in between.

There are so many problems with this, I don't even know where to start. I put the book down and massage my temples.

First of all: raisins in cookies are an abomination. Oatmeal cookies are good, but they should have chocolate chips, not raisins. Who the hell thinks raisins belong in oatmeal cookies?

Second of all: raisins and mocha don't go together at all. They clash. Isn't that obvious?

I sigh, then pick up the book and continue reading.

It doesn't matter if people think your inner ice cream sandwich is stupid, either because they are affronted by the very concept of having an inner ice cream sandwich, or because they don't like your ice cream and cookie choices. This is your ice cream sandwich. It should perfectly capture you, and you should treasure it. Don't let anyone melt your inner ice cream sandwich. Don't let people like Marvin Wong anywhere near your ice cream sandwich.

Uh-huh.

Lisa provides a list of cookies and ice cream flavors the reader could consider for their own ice cream sandwich, but she emphasizes that this is not a complete list, and it's up to you, the reader, to find your own inner truth.

Uh-huh.

Your flavors should be things that you like, and that represent you. Maybe your ice cream is chocolate chip cookie dough. Little chunks of sweet and raw passion. The obvious cookie pairing would be chocolate chip cookies, but dare to be different! How about double chocolate cookies? I think that adds an air of sophistication. Or perhaps peanut butter cookies because you have a nutty sense of humor?

I have no idea what she's going on about. It sounds like a bunch of bullshit to me.

Now I, personally, am not a fan of black sesame. But if you're mysterious and a little exotic, maybe this will work for you.

Exotic? Seriously?

Ugh.

I'm probably the only reason Lisa has even tried black sesame ice cream. I recall taking her to an Asian dessert place in the north end of the city, and she had a sundae with black sesame and mango ice cream.

I have a clear memory of that day. We sat at the back of the café, and it felt like the rest of the world just disappeared.

I don't expect to ever have a date like that again.

While we're speaking of exotic flavors, another option is green tea ice cream, which I tried once at an all-you-can-eat sushi restaurant.

Frankly, I don't think green tea and ice cream belong together, but perhaps this represents how you're an unusual combination!

If you need inspiration, visit a local ice cream parlor. Be bold, be brave, and order a triple scoop of things you've never tried before!

Uh-huh.

It rubs me the wrong way that the only two flavors of ice cream she doesn't like are black sesame and green tea. I feel personally attacked, even though I no longer eat ice cream. Also, I doubt most all-you-can-eat sushi restaurants serve very good green tea ice cream. Maybe she'd feel differently if she tried the green tea ice cream at Ginger Scoops.

I have a sip of beer and start reading again.

Now, you're probably wondering about Marvin Wong's inner ice cream sandwich...

Nope, not happening. I'm done with this crap for today.

I shut the book and rub my temples, trying to restore the brain cells I lost in the past half hour.

I don't have any plans for the evening. I texted Glenn earlier to see if he was around, but his son caught some awful bug from daycare, and now Glenn's sick, too. It'll just be me and my home entertainment system.

Well, that's not so bad. I don't actually mind spending Saturday nights alone.

My chest feels a little heavy at the thought, but this is my life, and I like it.

Really, I do.

It suits me, being alone most of the time.

And someday this week, I'll go to Ginger Scoops and get a few pints of ice cream, and...crap. I also need to get Michelle a birthday present. That totally slipped my mind.

What on earth should I get a six-year-old foodie?

[6]
CHLOE

It's eight o'clock on Wednesday, and nobody is in Ginger Scoops but me. I straighten the napkins for the zillionth time and sigh.

Business has been okay, but not quite as good as I'd hoped.

The chimes above the door tinkle, and to my surprise, Drew walks in. He's wearing jeans and a T-shirt, as well as a scowl. I didn't expect to see him until the weekend, and I certainly didn't expect to see him by himself.

"Hello," I say. "Fancy seeing you again."

"I'm going to be spending too much here," he grumbles. "My niece loves your ice cream."

"You've been looking after her a lot lately?"

He nods. "Every Saturday while my sister's at work."

"She seems like a sweet kid."

"She is." He manages a slight smile.

Aw. My skin prickles at that smile.

"But your niece isn't here today," I say.

"No. I've been tasked with getting ice cream for her birthday party." He sounds as enthusiastic as someone who's about to get a tooth pulled. "Do you sell pints?"

"We do! Just let me get the containers."

I scurry to the back and return with a stack of pints. Drew is the first person who's asked about take-home containers, and I can't help feeling excited.

"Alright, what do you want?" I ask.

He reads the list of twelve flavors on the blackboard, then throws up his arms. "Fuck, I don't know. I don't eat ice cream."

"Maybe you should try."

He scowls.

"Come on, it's just ice cream. It's not going to bite."

"I don't like it."

"Why not? Did you get hit by an ice cream truck as a child? Or did you have a particularly traumatic brain freeze?"

"No, it's nothing like that."

"I know what it is," I say. "You don't like happiness!"

"You're accusing me of not liking happiness?"

"Well, I don't know. You remind me of Oscar the Grouch."

"Because I'm green and furry and live in a trashcan?"

"Do you? I've never been to your place."

And now I can't help but imagine going home with Drew. He'd flick on the lights as soon as we walked in the door, then press me against the wall and kiss his way down my neck...

I don't know why I'm having these thoughts.

Except I do. He's handsome, and it's been a long time since I've been with anyone.

Drew looks around the room, and his gaze lingers on the corner with the rocking unicorn and the rainbow painted on the wall. He shakes his head.

Now I feel defensive. "Look, I know you think it looks like a unicorn threw up in here—"

"Strangely, that's exactly what I thought the first time I walked in."

"—but most people love ice cream. And do you know how many children have sat on that rocking unicorn since I opened this place? I'm going to buy a second one."

"I didn't always hate ice cream," he says. "Only in the past year."

Interesting. "What happened?"

"It makes me gag."

"Just all of a sudden, ice cream started making you gag?"

He nods but says nothing.

"Do you know why that happens?"

"Oh, I know exactly why."

I wait a few seconds, hoping he'll add something. We look at each other. His hair is a touch long, and there's a piece sticking up near his ear. I want to smooth it down.

I don't understand why I'm drawn to this man. He's grouchy. He hates ice cream.

And yet, he intrigues me, and it's not just because of his good looks.

It's almost like the air feels different when he's near me.

"Do you know the book *Embrace Your Inner Ice Cream Sandwich?*"

I get whiplash from the change in topic. Where's he going with this?

"Um, yeah," I say. "It's a pretty big book right now."

"My ex wrote it."

I stare at him for a moment, and then I burst into laughter. I can't help it. Drew dated a woman who wrote a book called *Embrace Your Inner Ice Cream Sandwich?*

"Are you serious?" I ask.

"Sadly, yes."

"Have you read it?"

"I just finished it."

"Is it a literary masterpiece?"

"I, uh, wouldn't go that far."

"Okay, so ice cream makes you gag now because it reminds you of your ex-girlfriend?"

"My ex-fiancée. She left me at the altar."

"Oh, Drew." I reach out to touch him, then pull my hand back.

"Anyway," he says, "it's probably obvious to you why I got left at the altar, seeing as I remind you of Oscar the Grouch. Lisa had some not-so-kind things to say about me in the book—there's a whole chapter on me. She even called me 'a cross between Eeyore and Oscar the Grouch on steroids'. Maybe you two would get along."

I can't help but chuckle. "I assume she didn't get your permission to write about you?"

"No, but what am I going to do? I haven't consulted a lawyer, but I have no interest in suing my ex-fiancée, plus most of what she said was…probably true." He says the last two words quietly. "Although she renamed me in the book, everyone in my life knows that Marvin Wong is me, of course, and she repeatedly mentions how I melted her inner ice cream sandwich."

"I may have to read this book for myself."

"Go ahead. Seems like it would be right up your alley."

"Actually, it sounds a bit silly to me."

He flashes me a brief smile that makes me feel warm and tingly. "I'm not heartbroken over her anymore. I just can't stomach ice cream."

"When was the last time you had some?"

"A year ago."

"Maybe things have changed. Are you sure you don't want to try something?" I gesture to the ice cream tubs. "Just a taste. Maybe chocolate-raspberry or Vietnamese coffee?"

He shakes his head.

Okay, I won't keep pushing him. "We still have to decide on some flavors for your niece's birthday party."

"Whatever you think will go with a chocolate ganache cake."

"She's having a chocolate ganache cake, not, I don't know, a Dora the Explorer cake?"

"Foodies do not typically ask for Dora the Explorer cakes for their birthdays, even if they're only six years old."

I remember her trying the green tea-strawberry ice cream and saying it needed more green tea. I smile.

In fact, Drew and I are both smiling stupidly at each other.

Too bad I've sworn off dating. He's kind of cute.

But even if I were interested in dating, he's probably super bitter after his ex-fiancée left him at the altar and then wrote about him in a bestselling book.

Not the sort of person I should want to date.

Back to ice cream. "I'm thinking...not ginger-lime, and not black sesame."

Drew snorts. "Definitely not black sesame. That's only appropriate if you're mysterious and a little exotic."

"What?" I recoil at that word. I hate it, but it's not like he's talking about *me*.

"That's how Lisa described black sesame ice cream in her book."

I'm definitely curious about this book, but I doubt I'd like it. I also don't want to actually pay money for it.

"How many flavors are you looking to buy?" I ask Drew.

"Two or three. I'm not sure. How much ice cream do eight little girls need? But if there's a little extra, that's fine. Probably best to go with three."

"How about passionfruit, chocolate-raspberry, and strawberry-lychee sorbet? It might be good to have a dairy-free one."

"Sure. You're the ice cream expert, not me."

I take the first pint and start scooping out passionfruit ice cream. If pints become popular—I hope they do!—then I'll get a little freezer for ready-to-go pints. But for now, I have to scoop them for customers from the ice cream tubs. I try to think of something to ask Drew while I'm working.

Why are you so handsome?

What do you look like under that T-shirt?

Instead, I keep my mouth shut, and Drew steps away from the counter and wanders around the store.

"Is this you in the photograph? When you were a little girl?" he asks.

I look up. "Yes. Me and my mother."

"You looked so much like Michelle."

"I did." She's not the only young girl I've met who has a similar background to mine—one white parent, one East Asian parent—but she's the only one who reminds me of my younger self.

Suddenly, I'm hit with a strange bundle of emotions. The fondness in Drew's words and expression as he speaks of his niece... It makes me want to smile. But I don't. I'm also thinking about my mother, wishing she could see this place. Wishing she were here to remark on how I didn't choose *exactly* the shade of pink paint that she would have chosen.

My mother liked to critique little things in my life. We'd argue a lot, but when it came down to it, I think she understood me better than anyone else.

Or maybe I'm wrong about that. Maybe I'm misremembering.

It's been five years.

What would we be like together now? How much would our relationship have changed?

I think we would have gotten along better as I got older; we wouldn't have had so many stupid disagreements, though I suspect she'd still critique my choice of paint color.

Yet, if my mother had lived, I doubt I would have opened Ginger Scoops.

For a moment, I hate that this place exists, I hate what it represents. Then I take a deep breath and drag my mind away from the could-have-beens. It's not productive to think of those.

"Chloe?" Drew is standing across the counter from me again. "Are you okay?"

"I'm fine."

He looks doubtful, but he's not pushing me to tell the truth, which makes me want to tell him.

"That picture...of my mom and me...my mother is dead." I can't seem to form a coherent sentence.

"I'm sorry, Chloe." He puts his hand on the counter, beside the cash register, as though offering comfort if I want to take it. I put down the ice cream scoop and place my right hand on top of his.

We say nothing for a long moment; we simply touch. He puts his other hand on top of mine and squeezes. His hands are warm and large and immensely comforting.

I can't help wanting more of this, but I slide my hand away and go back to scooping the chocolate-raspberry ice cream.

"Michelle asked if she would be as pretty as you when she grows up," he says, presumably in an effort to distract me.

"Do you think I'm pretty?"

Oops. The question just popped out of my mouth.

He raises his eyebrows, just slightly. "Objectively, you're very pretty."

"Objectively?"

"You have nice features. I'm sure most men would agree."

"Mm-hmm. I wasn't asking for an objective opinion, but a personal one."

I'm being a bit flirtatious. Huh. Flirting is not something I've done much of lately, and we were just talking about my mother a minute ago. This conversation is confusing the crap out of me.

"Personally, I think you're pretty."

He doesn't sound cocky and confident, unlike the man who tried to pick me up at a bar last month. But I'm pretty sure Drew isn't looking for a relationship right now.

Although that doesn't mean he's not looking for some fun in the bedroom...

My face heats, and we look at each other like two sixteen-year-old kids who have no idea what we're doing, and oh God, why do I find this so endearing?

"Anyway." He clears his throat, but his voice is still croaky afterward. "You were going to give me some strawberry-lychee sorbet?"

"Yes, yes. Of course." I grab the last pint and quickly scoop the sorbet into it.

It's been over six months since I've gone to bed with anyone. Hannah and I weren't in a relationship; we just slept together a few times. Before that, there was a one-night stand with a guy named Brett. Or was it Brent? I'm not sure, and I feel embarrassed for not remembering the name of a guy I slept with.

No, it was Brett. I'm pretty sure.

I remind myself that there's no shame in forgetting the name of a one-night stand.

Drew might look a touch awkward now, but I think if we actually went to bed together, he wouldn't be awkward it all.

I swallow and put the three pints on the counter. "Will that be everything for today? Would you like a coffee?"

"Not tonight," he says, "but I'd like to ask you a question."

Oh? Every inch of my skin feels very *aware* of his presence. Maybe he's going to ask if he can kiss me or take me back to his place after all.

"Your store and Michelle's bedroom have a similar aesthetic," he says. "Any suggestions for where I might, uh, buy her a birthday present?"

Totally not what I was expecting.

"There's a place on Queen West called Libby's Gifts," I say, trying to hide my disappointment. "That's where I got the stuffed alpacas." I point to a shelf along one wall of the store.

"Right. Somehow I never noticed the alpacas before."

"You were too overwhelmed by the rainbows and unicorns and pink walls."

"Something like that."

"Your niece's birthday party is this weekend, and you still haven't gotten her a present? You're a little behind, aren't you, Drew?" I tease.

"I got her main present on Sunday, but I thought I'd get her something else, something that's actually...cute and intended for children."

"What have you gotten her already?"

"A pasta maker and some expensive olive oil to have with crusty bread."

I stare at him. "You got your niece a pasta maker? A real one, not a kids' toy?"

He nods. "Like I said, she's a real foodie. She'll like it, trust me."

I'm a little skeptical, but he knows her better than me.

I ring up the three pints of ice cream. Drew hands over his credit card, and I slide it into the machine. As I'm giving it back to him, I notice the last name on his card.

"Lum," I say. "The only other person I knew with that name was a friend of my late grandmother's. They were from the same area in China." I can't help the hope from creeping into my voice, can't help desperately wanting that connection, but for all I know, it could be a meaningless coincidence. Perhaps it's common in many parts of China—I know nothing about names.

"My dad's family is from Toisan," he says as he enters his pin number.

"My mother's family, too! You speak the language?"

"I don't, but my dad does. Kind of. He was born here."

"Like my mom."

I know it's stupid, but this makes me happy. Toronto has an enormous Chinese population, and I had many Chinese friends growing up, but their family backgrounds were all different from my own. When I meet someone who is Chinese and over the age of fifty and doesn't have an accent—someone who sounds like they grew up in Canada, I mean—I feel like we're related.

Which isn't *quite* as stupid as it sounds, since most of the earlier Chinese immigrants to Canada, like Drew's father's family, were from Sze Yup, the Four Counties—Toisan being one of them.

"And your mother?" I ask.

"She's from Hong Kong. She came here for university, where she met my father."

I nod and resist the urge to hug him. I feel a special bond with him now. It's something I crave, now that my mother and Chinese grandparents are gone.

I put the ice cream pints in a bag and smile at him. "You have to keep ice cream in the freezer. Just so you know. Since, from the sounds of it, you are not particularly familiar with ice cream." I try to keep my voice light.

He narrows his eyes at me, but I can see the amusement dancing in them.

"I'm not a total idiot when it comes to ice cream," he says.

"Maybe I'll convince you to try some one of these days."

"Don't hold your breath."

I smile at him and he heads to the door. When he opens it, he waves at me before walking out into the night. He doesn't smile, and although he reminds me of Oscar the Grouch, I feel a strange lightness in my chest.

DREW

THURSDAY AFTER WORK, I head to Libby's Gifts, which is near Trinity Bellwoods Park.

When I open the door, I look around in horror. This place is unbearably cutesy. Like, Ginger Scoops is a little over the top, but this place is...wow.

And then I smile when I think of Chloe telling me about this store. It was exactly what I had in mind when I asked for a recommendation for a place to buy Michelle a gift.

Well, I'll take a look around and hopefully be out of here in five minutes, otherwise I might have nightmares of giant kittens, puppies, and unicorns chasing me through an enchanted forest.

I shiver at the thought.

There's a large shelf devoted to Hello Kitty, the popularity of which I do not understand. There are Hello Kitties in every size, from keychains to stuffed ones that are almost as big as me. One Hello Kitty is carrying a cupcake; another is riding a unicorn.

I move on. I find cutesy notebooks, cutesy magnets, and cutesy socks, but nothing is quite right.

In the greeting card section, there are several intricate pop-up cards, including one of a couple embracing on a bridge near a

Chinese pavilion and a willow tree. I stare at it for a moment. If I had a girlfriend...

What the hell?

I don't want to be in a relationship. I'm done with relationships. Given my luck, if I were to start a relationship now, the woman would probably leave me at the altar and then write a book that would ruin both chocolate and beer for me.

I'm really not creative.

But I bet Chloe is, including in the bedroom...

I slam the door on that train of thought.

I move away from the romantic pop-up cards and find one with a mother and baby elephant, plus another with a castle that looks like it escaped from a Disney movie. After a minute of indecision, I decide to buy the latter for Michelle.

Next, I come across a section of stuffed animals, including an alpaca with a little blue hat jauntily perched on its head. Or is that a llama? I tilt my head and regard it for a moment.

No, definitely an alpaca.

I pull it off the shelf and move farther into the store, where I come across some amigurumi.

Yes, I actually know what amigurumi is. Back in university, I used to date a woman who was obsessed with them. She'd crochet tiny cute animals for stress relief. During exam period, she crocheted me a pair of giraffes.

I dumped her as soon as exam period was over. Not because of the amigurumi giraffes, which I kept because it seemed like a crime to throw them out and I'm not completely heartless, but because I'd fallen out of love with her.

She also insisted on teaching me how to crochet, and I might still have my ugly attempt at a puppy somewhere in my closet.

But here in Libby's Gifts, there's a perfectly-crocheted elephant, as well as a series of other animals. Lions, tigers, bears, moose, turtles and a very intricate peacock.

"Can I help you?"

I jump in surprise when I hear a woman's voice behind me.

"Um…" I'm tongue-tied. Speechless in horror at the fact that someone has found me carefully examining an amigurumi peacock, in a shop that looks like some kind of utopia for people who are high on sunshine and kawaii.

"What are you looking for?"

I put the peacock back on the shelf. "I'm shopping for my niece. She's turning six."

"Perhaps she could use some glitter pens? Or a Hello Kitty lunchbox?"

"Actually, she already has one of those," I mutter. "I'll take a look around and let you know if I have any questions, okay?"

She walks away, and I discover a collection of amigurumi food next to the animals. There's a hamburger, a carrot, a cabbage, an apple, an eggplant…

Hmm. Perhaps my foodie niece would appreciate some amigurumi fruit and vegetables. I pick up the eggplant, then notice the peach beside it.

I choke and push thoughts of Chloe out of my mind as I shove the eggplant back on the shelf.

Deciding I've had enough of amigurumi, I head toward the cash register, though I get distracted by the sticker selection— just kidding—and place my alpaca and pop-up card on the counter.

"Are you sure I can't interest you in some glitter pens?" the woman asks.

"Uh, no, that's quite alright."

"What about this?"

It's a little box with a cute hedgehog on top, and inside is some stationery with woodland creatures, plus some small pencil crayons, two strawberry erasers, gel pens, and a hedgehog pencil sharpener.

You know what? I can't deal with any more of this store. I

need to get out of here ASAP before I turn into Totoro. "Sure, whatever, I'll buy the hedgehog stationery set, too."

~

When I arrive at Adrienne's on Saturday morning, Michelle runs up to me. She's wearing a blue party dress and a blue ribbon in her hair.

"Happy birthday," I say as she hugs my waist.

"Hi, Uncle Drew." Then she drops her voice. "I'm supposed to pretend to be more interested in you than your presents."

I laugh.

Adrienne enters the front hall and regards all the packages I've placed on the bench by the door. She had to switch shifts with someone so she wouldn't miss her daughter's birthday. "You're spoiling her."

I shrug. "Isn't that what I'm supposed to do?"

"Can I open them now, Mommy?" Michelle looks up at her mother with wide, pleading eyes.

"You can open them after lunch, which I hope your uncle brought with him."

I hold up the bag of sushi. "It's here."

Apparently, Michelle wanted a make-your-own-sushi party with her friends, but Adrienne managed to convince her that a paint-your-own-unicorn party was a better idea. I glance into the living room, where a folding table has been set up. It's covered with newspaper, and there are eight unicorn figurines, maybe six inches high.

This is the party I will help supervise this afternoon. How lovely.

"Okay, Michelle," Adrienne says. "Uncle Drew has seen you in your party dress. Now you can go upstairs and get changed for lunch."

"Why can't you wear your party dress for lunch?" I ask.

Michelle sighs, as though her mother is being totally unfair. "Mommy says soy sauce and party dresses do not mix. She also says that paint and party dresses do not mix."

"Your mother is very wise."

"Why are you taking her side? You're supposed to be cool."

"You'll think I'm very cool once you open your presents."

"Mommy, can't I open them *now*?"

Just then, the front door opens, and a male voice says, "Where's the birthday girl?"

Adrienne's mouth opens in surprise.

"Daddy!" Michelle shrieks and rushes toward her father. Nathan hugs Michelle then swings her into his arms, and I most certainly do not feel my eyes getting a bit misty.

But for a split second, I wish I had this life.

I thought I would, once upon a time. Lisa and I had decided we'd start trying to have kids after we'd been married for a year.

Of course, that was before she climbed out a window at the church.

Why she didn't just walk out the door, I'm not sure.

"You didn't tell me you were coming." Adrienne kisses her husband, who is still carrying Michelle, on the cheek.

"I decided at the last minute and thought I'd surprise you."

There are dark circles under his eyes, but he looks happy.

Nathan puts Michelle down. "I bought you a present, but I didn't get a chance to wrap it." He reaches into his pocket and pulls out a small gray box.

Michelle opens it up and gasps. Inside is a silver necklace with a heart pendant. "It's like grown-up jewelry!"

He chuckles. "Yes. Grown-up jewelry. Because you're a big girl now."

"Put it on for me, Daddy!"

He clasps the necklace around her neck, and she hugs him again.

Feeling a little superfluous in this family moment, I head to the kitchen and get out some plates for the sushi.

~

After lunch, Adrienne says I can leave since Nathan is there to help with the party, but I decide to stay. Not because I'm particularly excited about watching eight little girls decorate unicorns, but I'm here, so why not? What else am I going to do today? Plus, I admit I'm a little tempted by that chocolate ganache cake.

However, one of the little girls came down with a fever this morning, so there's an extra unicorn figurine, and Michelle insists I decorate it myself.

So here I am, staring at my unicorn figurine and wondering what the hell I should do. I finally decide on something simple: I'll paint it white with a purple mane. Then I'll give it to Michelle, since I don't need it for myself.

I grab some white paint and start working on my unicorn. The girl beside me has also decided to go for something simple. She appears to be a Goth in training, and she's painting the entire thing black.

I'm so intently focused on painting my unicorn—ha!—that I don't notice there's a problem until I hear some shrieks. (In truth, I was daydreaming about the beer I plan to have when I'm home and no longer surrounded by seven six-year-olds.) One of the girls has dumped an entire jar of glitter on her unicorn.

"Ava used all the glitter!" one of the girls whines, and two others join in.

I look around frantically for Adrienne or Nathan, but they are nowhere to be found, so it looks like I'll have to deal with this myself. Great.

"The glitter is for everyone," I say. "You have to share. Sharing is caring."

Goddammit, where did that come from?

Ava looks at me as though I'm speaking a foreign language.

I sigh. "Look, most of the glitter didn't stick to Ava's unicorn. I can fix it, okay?"

I shake the unicorn to rid it of excess glitter, then sweep the pound of glitter on the newspaper back into the jar. The other girls are content with this, and I go back to painting my unicorn. Since my fingers are covered in glitter, I get some on my unicorn, but that's okay. It's a fucking unicorn.

After I finish with the white paint, I reach for the purple and start painting the tail, then the mane. Satisfied, I push it away from me and look around the table. Goth Girl has just finished painting her unicorn black, and everyone else is still busily working on making their unicorns a mess of colors and glitter.

Michelle looks up at me. "You're already done, Uncle Drew?"

I nod.

She shakes her head, a look of deep disappointment on her face. "Your unicorn is so boring. It only has two colors."

I'm tempted to point out that mine is still more colorful than Goth Girl's unicorn, but I'm not six, so I don't say that.

"It has glitter," I say instead, slightly defensive.

"Not very much glitter."

"Fine. I'll give it a tattoo."

Now Michelle is intrigued.

I grab the pink paint. The white part of my unicorn is dry, and I quickly add a pink heart to its ass. It's a very finely-shaped heart, if I do say so myself.

"There," I say. "It now has a heart tattoo on its...bum."

"I want a heart tattoo on my unicorn's bum!" Michelle says. "Can you paint it for me?"

"You can do it yourself."

"But I can't make the heart as nice as you can."

"Alright," I grumble.

Ten minutes later, I have painted a pink heart on every unicorn's bum. Even Goth Girl's unicorn. I was surprised she asked for one, but perhaps she felt left out, or she liked the thought of her unicorn having a tattoo, even if it was a pink heart.

Adrienne enters the room, a glass of red wine in hand, just as another fight breaks out over the glitter. Fortunately, my sister handles this one. Nathan enters the room a moment later, and I figure I can take a breather. I find the bottle of wine on the kitchen counter, pour myself a generous glass, and ruminate on the fact that my life now involves decorating unicorns, buying stuffed alpacas, and being a regular patron of a cutesy ice cream shop.

～

The chocolate ganache cake is amazing, though it's wasted on most of the party guests, who'd be more impressed if it had My Little Pony decorations. But it's still chocolate cake, and they are happy to eat it, as well as the ice cream. The strawberry-lychee sorbet proves particularly popular and I can't wait to tell Chloe about this.

Interesting that she's on my mind so much.

I, of course, do not have any ice cream. I may have painted a unicorn at a six-year-old's birthday party, but I draw the line at eating ice cream.

After the kids leave, it's blessedly quiet in the house, but I feel a bit of a headache coming on after all the earlier excitement. I'll wait for Michelle to open my presents, then leave.

Michelle begins with the stuffed alpaca, followed by the hedgehog stationery set. She likes both of these, but she's not as impressed with the bottle of olive oil as I'd hoped.

Seriously, what was I thinking, buying a bottle of good olive oil for a child just because she's a foodie? She's only six.

Next, she unwraps the pasta maker and squeals in delight when she sees the box.

I can't help but smile.

"Mommy, it's a real pasta maker, not like the fake one you got me at Christmas!"

I turn to Adrienne. "A fake pasta maker?"

"I got her a Play-Doh one. She wasn't impressed."

"Let's use it tonight!" Michelle starts opening the box.

"Tomorrow, honey," Nathan says, patting her shoulder. "It might take a little while to set it up and make the dough, but we can try it before I leave."

"You have to leave tomorrow?" Michelle's chin wobbles.

He nods. "I only came back for the weekend."

"I don't want you to leave. Mommy made the grossest dinner last night. Food is so much better when you make it."

"Gee, thanks," Adrienne says.

"But it's true!" Michelle protests.

"I know. Your dad is a much better cook than me."

"I can't wait until I'm big enough to use the kitchen without an adult. Will I be old enough when I'm seven?"

"We'll talk about it later, baby."

Michelle comes over to me. "Thank you for the pasta maker. It's the best."

As my niece throws her arms around my neck, I can't help longing, once more, for this life. A life I gave up on years ago, when I found myself alone in my bed on the night that should have been my wedding night.

For years, I didn't bother wishing for a wife and family.

But now, I grudgingly admit that it might be kind of nice.

[8]
CHLOE

On Sunday afternoon, I scoop ice cream and ring up orders continuously for an hour. It's good to be busy. When there's finally a lull, I look around the small shop and smile. There are four families and two couples sitting inside, and another family plus a group of teenagers on the patio. Some are enjoying their ice cream in a cone or bubble waffle; others have it in a cup. Everyone looks happy.

This is what I dreamed of.

A year after my mother died, I was working thirty hours a week as a waitress at an English pub in the downtown core. I couldn't summon the energy or interest to go back to university. I felt lost, adrift, and the one person I could have talked to about it…she was gone.

I read a bunch of self-help books, which somehow left me feeling even more broken, and then I read one that suggested writing down a list of things that make you happy and working from there.

I wrote "Things that make me happy" at the top of a sheet of paper and stared at it for five minutes. Surely I should be able to write *something*.

I added "ice cream" and "chocolate" as a joke, so I could at least have something on the paper. Then I stared at those two items for a long time. It seemed ridiculous that I couldn't think of anything else.

I wasn't in a good place at the time, and I'd coped by trying to feel as little as possible. I couldn't make myself entirely numb, but I did my best. I could deal with feeling little joy if it took the edge off my grief, though I still put on a cheerful face in public.

But as I stared at the words on that sheet of paper, I started to feel the stirrings of…something. I'd heard about a new ice cream parlor on Eglinton called Fancy Schmancy Ice Cream, and they made interesting flavors, like pear-vanilla-peppercorn. I went there on one of my days off. It's a simple place with white walls, pale wood furniture, and tubs of ice cream in a multitude of colors. Somehow, I found a strange sense of peaceful joy while I sat by the window and licked my ice cream cone. I thought of the days my mom would take me to the ice cream parlor in the summer when I was a child. And when I thought of my mother while sitting in Fancy Schmancy Ice Cream, I could smile at my memories. It was tinged with sadness, but I didn't feel an unbearable ache in my chest that made me want to shriek at the top of my lungs. Instead, my grief felt manageable.

I imagined opening my own ice cream parlor, and even though the idea seemed preposterous, for the first time in ages, I was the tiniest bit motivated. I treasured that motivation—I'd forgotten what it was like to actually want something that wasn't a hundred percent impossible, like my mother coming back from the dead.

Fancy Schmancy Ice Cream wasn't hiring, but I got a job for summer weekends at another ice cream parlor, not far from home. I loved seeing all the kids' smiling faces, but I realized that I didn't simply want to scoop ice cream that arrived on a truck. I wanted to make my own.

When the summer was over, I begged the owner of Fancy

Schmancy Ice Cream for an informal apprenticeship of sorts. Johann is a burly man of about forty who fancies plaid shirts and not shaving, and eventually, he said he would teach me. I have no idea why he agreed, but he did, and I watched—and offered what little assistance I could—as he developed new flavors over the winter. The following summer, he paid me to scoop ice cream part-time, and I helped him make the ice cream, too.

And now, I have my own ice cream parlor. It's such a happy place. Everyone is always happy when they're going out for ice cream.

Except for Drew, though I think he's happy to put a smile on his niece's face, even if he refuses to indulge in ice cream himself and has a tendency to scowl.

Still, I grin when I think of him.

It's five thirty, and we'll be closing soon. Nobody's come in for twenty minutes. Valerie is in the back, so it's just me at the counter when a middle-aged man and woman come in. The woman reads the list of flavors, then looks at me with a puzzled expression.

"Do you have any questions about the flavors?" I ask.

"I'll have a sugar cone with the chocolate-raspberry."

"I'll have a regular cone with the Vietnamese coffee."

The Vietnamese coffee has been popular today. We're at the bottom of the tub now. As I'm reaching down with the ice cream scoop, the woman says, "What *are* you, dear?"

I am a human.

I am a woman.

I am the owner of Ginger Scoops.

But none of those are the answers she's looking for. Despite the vague question, I know exactly what she's asking. Normally, I might give one of the above answers, but this is my business and

I'm worried she'll leave a Yelp or Google review that says "rude service."

I finish scooping the Vietnamese coffee ice cream, hand the cone over to the man, and start on the chocolate-raspberry.

"My father is white," I say, my jaw tense. "My mother was Asian. Her family came from China."

"Ah. That explains it."

"It" being my appearance, I assume. I half-expect her to tell me that I look "exotic." Barf.

"Do you speak Chinese?" she asks.

"No."

I think she's disappointed in me, and I brace myself for a lecture on how it's important for me to be in touch with my heritage, etc., like it's any of her business.

But, thankfully, she says nothing more.

I hand over her cone with a rigid smile, then ring up their order. Once they head out into the sunshine, the tension in my body slowly begins to dissipate. I don't understand why white people think I owe them answers to such questions when they don't even know my name.

Valerie comes out from the back room. "You look like you need a drink."

"I just got asked 'What are you?' again."

I used to assume that I got these questions because I'm mixed race and slightly ambiguous-looking, but a few years ago, I discovered that Asian people who don't look like they have mixed ancestry get this, too. I don't understand why it's of critical importance that a stranger know whether someone's family is from Japan or China.

"Ugh," Valerie says. "You should have said you were an iguana or something."

I chuckle. "Why? Am I green and scaly today?"

"No, you look good. For real. Your boobs look great in that shirt."

"Why, thank you."

"And you'll get to pour alcohol down your throat real soon."

Sarah, Valerie, and I sometimes get together after we close our stores at six o'clock on Sundays. Monday is the only day of the week that Happy As Pie and Ginger Scoops are closed, so Sunday night is like Friday night for us.

By seven thirty, we're sitting around Sarah's kitchen table, drinking large glasses of red wine and eating chicken pot pie and curried lamb pie. The pie is courtesy of Sarah, of course. These are today's leftovers from her shop.

"That shirt looks really good on you," she says to me. "The burgundy suits you, and it makes your boobs look great."

"That's exactly what I said." Valerie laughs. "Too bad Drew comes in on Saturdays, not Sundays. Although, come to think of it, I didn't see him yesterday. Or did he come in when I was having lunch, and you didn't tell me?" She looks at me, eyebrows raised.

"He didn't come in. Yesterday was his niece's birthday party."

"How did you know that? He told you last week?"

"No, he came in on Wednesday and bought some pints for the party."

Valerie and Sarah exchange a look. I stuff a bite of curried lamb pie in my mouth, then wash it down with some wine.

"He's just a guy," I say.

"A super attractive guy," Valerie says. "And he keeps coming back, even though he hates ice cream."

"Because his niece likes it."

"I think it has something to do with *you*."

My face heats. "I, uh, discovered why he hates ice cream. His ex-fiancée wrote that *Embrace Your Inner Ice Cream Sandwich* book that's been getting so much buzz."

"For fuck's sake," Valerie says. "There's a book called *Embrace Your Inner Ice Cream Sandwich*? What the hell is wrong with people?"

"I've heard of it," Sarah says. "My mother told me to read it. I told her no, but that if she found a book called *Embrace Your Inner Pie Filling*, I might be tempted."

Valerie turns to me. "You're the one who reads self-help books. Have you read this one?"

I shake my head.

I'm no longer desperately trying to figure out my life. Instead, I read books about running a small business and stuff like that. Occasionally, if I have time, I read novels.

"Anyway," I continue, "Drew's ex—who left him at the altar—skewered his personality in the book, so he doesn't have good associations with ice cream anymore."

Valerie doubles over in laughter.

"You have to change his mind!" Sarah says. "Time for the ultimate ice cream seduction." She pauses. "Or maybe his personality really is that bad."

"You haven't dated in a while, Chloe," Valerie points out. "No men, no women."

I raise my eyebrows and attempt a mischievous smile. "That's what you think."

It's easier to pretend I might have a secret lover than to tell her the truth, which is that I don't seem to be able to do intimacy anymore, that I never feel fully *present* in any kind of relationship.

I have the same problem with friends, too. I'm friendly, and I reached out and got to know Sarah earlier this year. But even when I'm enjoying wine and pie with Sarah and Valerie—seriously, who wouldn't enjoy this?—I don't feel like I can give a hundred percent of myself. Like I always feel a little isolated, even when I'm laughing and having fun.

With my family, it's the same way. There's this barrier that prevents me from being fully there, though with them, there's the race issue, too.

I never truly feel like I can talk to people, if that makes sense.

Though the other night when Drew came into Ginger Scoops, I felt a sliver of connection that I hadn't felt in a long time.

Or maybe that's just my imagination.

"Chloe!" Valerie says. "What are you hiding from me?" Although she doesn't say so, I can tell she's a little miffed that I might not be telling her everything about my life. I've known her since we had grade nine French together.

"I'm just kidding," I say. "I don't have time for Drew. I'm focused on making Ginger Scoops a success." That's what I always say.

"Wear that shirt next Saturday," Sarah says, "just in case. Though perhaps you should read *Embrace Your Inner Ice Cream Sandwich* and see exactly what his ex says about him."

"Frankly," Valerie says, "I wouldn't trust anyone who talks about embracing their inner ice cream sandwich. She sounds flaky to me. Even flakier than this delicious pie." She points at her curried lamb pie with her fork, then turns to me. "But you don't need to fall in love with him. Sex without love is better. Love is messy—I don't need that shit. Men are pricks, but they have their uses."

Sarah, who is happily dating Josh, looks like she's about to protest, but then—wisely, I might add—decides otherwise. I'm not in the mood for one of Valerie's rants.

She has good reasons for feeling the way she does, though.

"I bet Drew will be up for a one-night stand if you ask real sweetly," Valerie says.

My face heats, both from embarrassment and desire. It does sound rather appealing, even though one-night stands haven't done it for me lately.

I decide to wear the burgundy shirt next Saturday.

"Alright," Sarah says, "time for dessert." She takes a container of my green tea ice cream out of the freezer and brings over half a pie.

"What kind is this?" Valerie asks.

"Coconut."

"Mm," I say. "That sounds good."

"Yeah, I really think this will work."

For whatever reason, Sarah has been keen on finding the perfect pie to accompany my green tea ice cream for our pie à la mode specials.

"Do you want to dump all the ice cream on the pie and eat from the pan?" she asks.

I shake my head. "No, this sounds amazing, and I'm determined to have my share. I don't want to risk Valerie eating two-thirds of it."

"Hey!" Valerie says. "I'm not that much of a pig."

"Remember what happened the last time we ordered pizza?"

"Fine, fine," she mutters, waving her hand away from her.

Sarah cuts the pie into three equal pieces, put them on plates, and scoops green tea ice cream on top of each.

"Oh my God," I say after the first bite. It's not quite as good as the chocolate tart and Vietnamese coffee ice cream, but pretty damn close. I turn to Sarah. "This hits the spot. I was in a bad mood at the end of the workday because a customer came up to me and asked, 'What are you?'"

Sarah frowns. "What was she referring to?"

Right. Sarah is white. She's not familiar with that question.

My father is probably unaware that it happens, too, despite marrying an Asian woman, despite his biracial daughter.

"She wanted to know my racial background," I say. "Some people ask where I'm from instead. When I say 'Canada,' they ask where my parents are from, and I say 'Canada,' again. It completely blows their minds that not all Asians are immigrants."

"People are dumb," Sarah says simply.

"Tell me about it," Valerie says around a mouthful of pie.

I'm about to tell my friends about the time my father told me he never thought of my mother as Chinese, but instead I stuff my mouth with green tea ice cream. I don't even know how to articulate all my complicated feelings, plus it seems like a stupid thing to be sensitive about.

I pour myself more wine instead.

～

My father deposits a steak on my plate, and I help myself to some grilled asparagus and peppers. It's Monday, my day off. I've gone to his house—my childhood home—for dinner. Just the two of us, filling only half the kitchen table.

"How's work?" I ask him.

He tells me about one of the cases he's working on, and I pay enough attention so that I can interject questions here and there. His job is a safe topic.

Mine? Not so much.

But, inevitably, we come around to that subject.

"How's the ice cream business?" he asks.

"It's doing okay," I say.

"What's your bestselling flavor?"

Ah, such a nice, innocuous question.

"Vietnamese coffee. I have to make another batch tomorrow."

"Huh. Vietnamese coffee. Maybe your grandmother would like that."

"Are you going to bring her soon?" I ask.

"Actually, I suggested we go on Saturday, but she said she was busy."

"Busy? What on earth is she busy with, other than church?"

"I don't know." He smiles faintly, and that makes me smile, too. For once, I can pretend there's no distance between us. I can pretend he isn't completely vexed with my life choices.

To my surprise, he doesn't bring up dentistry at all. Not during dinner, not when we have tea and half-heartedly watch the NHL playoffs afterward. Not when he shows me how well the lilac tree in the backyard is doing.

But I don't kid myself that he's changed his opinion on what I should do with my life. It's nice to not be arguing with each other, but it seems a little fake.

When I'm ready to leave, he gives me a couple containers of chickpea salad "so you don't end up eating ice cream for lunch."

"Don't worry, Dad, I never eat ice cream for lunch."

He gives me a look.

"Really," I say. "Though sometimes I eat pie. My friend owns a pie store across the street. She has curried lamb pie, chicken pot pie—things like that."

"Make sure you get enough iron. Your mother had problems with anemia, and I don't know if that's hereditary, but—"

"I know, you've told me before."

Dad never used to check up on me like this—he left that to my mother—but now it's just the two of us.

"Are you going to the cemetery on Sunday?" he asks.

Sunday would have been my mother's fifty-sixth birthday. I'm a little surprised he said something about it.

"No," I say.

"That's fine." He puts a hand on my shoulder. "Whatever works for you. You can grieve however you need to grieve."

I swallow. I wish he had that opinion about other parts of my life.

"Are you going?" I ask.

"I don't think so. I went for our wedding anniversary."

That was at the end of April, and I feel bad that it totally slipped my mind. I should have called him.

We say our goodbyes, leaving so many things left unsaid.

DREW

"Daycares are breeding grounds for disease," Glenn says. "I swear, every other week, Tommy picks up something new, and then Radhika or I have to stay home with him, and sometimes one of us gets sick, too. I've been sick five times this year, and it's only May."

We're sitting in a pub on College, one of the ones we used to go to back when we were in university. Glenn Chalmers is one of my friends from engineering school. He works as an engineer now, while I went on to get a masters in financial math and work for a bank. His wife, Radhika, is also an engineer, in addition to running a successful blog about food in Toronto.

"Yeah, I've heard that about daycare," I say. "When your kid starts daycare, be prepared for lots of sick days."

Glenn leans forward. "At first, Radhika was the one taking all the sick days, and I didn't think anything of it. But then she pointed out that really, I ought to be staying home sometimes, too—it's not like my job is more important than hers. So I stayed home one day with Tommy, and my boss was totally confused as to why *I* would have to miss work because my son was sick." He shakes his head. "We're so conditioned to think women should always be the ones making sacrifices for the kids."

"Yeah, that's true." And it's a problem.

"You seeing anyone?" he asks with a smile.

"Nope."

"You gotta work on that, man."

Glenn says this every time. Always the exact same phrase. *You gotta work on that, man.* But since he never dwells on it, I don't mind. It's not like he wants to swap stories of misery about marriage, which I think is why some people tell me that I should get married. Glenn is generally a happy guy—the opposite of what people say about me—and he seems content with life, his eighteen-month-old son's frequent sickness aside.

Rather than smoothly moving on to a discussion about the Blue Jays or NHL playoffs as he usually would, he says, "You haven't dated much since Lisa. You're over her, aren't you?"

"Of course I am."

"The whole thing was unfortunate." Glenn was standing next to me in the church when I learned that my bride had escaped through a window. "You're better off without her, though."

"Yeah, I am." I pause. "I read the whole book. Finally."

"Did you?" He grins. "And have you embraced your inner ice cream sandwich?"

"Oh, yeah. It's fucking miraculous how much my mindset changed once I embraced the fact that my ice cream sandwich is oatmeal-raisin cookies—"

"Hold on a second. Raisins in cookies are an abomination."

"—filled with cotton candy ice cream." I chuckle. "You're right, raisins don't belong in cookies."

We talk a little more about cookies and beer and other things, and then, before it's even nine o'clock, we take our leave.

Back in university, our night would just be getting started at nine on a Friday, but now we're old men who like to be in bed before midnight and don't fancy having hangovers the next day. I nursed two pints of beer, and although I can feel that I've been drinking, I'm nowhere close to being drunk.

Glenn heads to the subway, and I walk east to my condo. It's starting to rain, but they predicted that in the forecast, so I've got my trusty umbrella with me. It's a pink Hello Kitty umbrella with ears sticking out of the top.

Just kidding. It's a plain black umbrella. Why the fuck would I have anything else?

I did, however, see an array of cutesy animal umbrellas at Libby's Gifts last week, and I couldn't help thinking of Chloe skipping down the street and holding a flamingo umbrella.

Don't ask.

All of a sudden, the rain changes from moderate to a torrential downpour. My umbrella isn't enough, not in this heavy rain, not with the stupid wind blowing the rain against my chest. I duck under an awning. Maybe it'll only be really heavy for a few minutes and I can wait it out.

From my quasi-dry position under the awning of a Chinese seafood restaurant, I look up to see where I am.

I'm on Baldwin Street.

For fuck's sake.

Why am I on Baldwin? It's not out of the way, true, but it's not how I'd usually walk home. Why did my feet take me here?

Not only am I on Baldwin, but Ginger Scoops is just two doors down, and before I know what I'm doing, I've walked to the ice cream shop and opened the door.

Nobody's here but me and Chloe.

"We're closing in a few minutes," she says cheerily as she straightens the tables. "But if you..." She trails off when she notices it's me. "Hi, Drew."

I don't know why I'm here.

I mean, I do, but I don't.

"Would you like a coffee?" she asks.

"No, it's too late for coffee."

"Tea?"

"Sure. Tea would be great."

"Sit down and I'll bring it over to you."

I take a seat at a table by the window and watch the rain hammering the sidewalks. But even though my gaze is in the opposite direction of Chloe, I'm very much aware of her presence.

She returns a minute later with two cups of tea and sits across from me. Someone else could come in at any moment to escape the storm, but for now, it's just us.

It feels momentous.

Although I haven't really dated since the wedding that never happened, I can't deny that I'm drawn to her, even though we're nothing alike.

"I was nearby, and I thought I'd wait out the rain here," I explain.

She nods. "It's really coming down out there. You look a little wet."

I lean my umbrella against a chair, then bring the cup of tea up to my mouth, even though it's too hot to drink. I sniff it instead.

"Oolong," she says. "I hope that's okay."

"It is. Thank you."

We look at each other.

Finally, she breaks the silence. "How was your niece's birthday party? Did she like the ice cream?"

"She did. The strawberry-lychee was particularly popular with the under-seven set."

Chloe smiles. "Did you get anything at Libby's Gifts?"

"Oh my God. That store."

"You felt like you were bombarded by cuteness?"

"Yeah. But I got Michelle a stuffed alpaca and a hedgehog stationery set, which she loved. She also loved the pasta maker. My sister sent me a picture of the first thing she made. With help, of course." I pull out my phone and show Chloe a close-up of the pasta carbonara. Next, there's a picture of Michelle grinning as she holds up the dish.

Chloe leans closer to me to look at the photo. She smells of lavender.

"What did you do at the birthday party?" she asks.

Distracted by her nearness, it takes me a moment to find my voice. "It was a paint-your-own unicorn figurine party."

"That sounds awesome."

"I knew you'd think that. It reminded me of you."

She raises an eyebrow. "You were thinking about me at your niece's birthday party?"

"With the ice cream and the unicorns…sure. Yes. I was."

"Mm."

I don't know what the *mm* means. I don't know anything right now, except that I want to be here. With her.

"I got to paint a unicorn, too," I tell her. "There was an extra one, and Michelle insisted." I flip through the photos on my phone. "Here."

She regards the picture of my white-and-purple unicorn and chuckles. "Oh, man. I wish I'd been there."

I wish she'd been there, too, but I don't say that.

"I borrowed your ex-fiancée's book from the library," she says. "I'm on chapter two."

"So you haven't been introduced to Marvin Wong yet."

"No, not yet, but I'm looking forward to that part."

"I'm sure you are."

"I also read an Oscar the Grouch book while I was at the library. You do have a startling resemblance to him. It's uncanny."

I give her my best scowl, and when she laughs, she slaps her hand against my knee…and leaves it there. I can feel the warmth of her hand through my jeans, and God, I want it against my bare skin.

Why her?

I don't know.

It feels like we're in our own little world. Outside, it's dark and rain is pelting the road, but in here, in this brightly-lit ice cream shop, we're safe.

Although this doesn't exactly feel "safe" to me.

I've done this before. I met a girl at a restaurant, we had mutual friends. We flirted all evening, and then I offered to walk her home, and we kissed on her doorstep. I took her out for ice cream sandwiches the next day. It lasted four years until it all went to shit.

Right now, it feels the same as that, but different, in a way, though I can't describe how.

Chloe stands up, closes the blinds, and flips the sign from "open" to "closed."

"It's nine o'clock," she says.

"Are you kicking me out?"

"No." But rather than coming back to the table, she goes around the counter and comes back with a spoon containing my nemesis.

Ice cream.

"I take it this is for me," I say.

"You've been in here four times, and you've yet to try a bite of ice cream. I think we need to change that. Just a bite, nothing more. On the house."

"How magnanimous of you," I mutter, "giving away a tiny sample for free."

"It's matcha cheesecake." She sits down and holds the spoon up to my mouth. Her face is close to mine, and my gaze shifts from her dark eyes to her cute and slightly upturned nose, then down to her lips, which are widened in a slight smile. My skin heats.

"No, thank you," I say.

"What about chocolate-raspberry? You said you like chocolate, right?"

"I think I'll pass."

"Hong Kong milk tea is our newest flavor."

"Chloe, I don't want any goddamn ice cream."

"Fine." She frowns. "I won't force you."

"I want…"

I lean forward and brush my fingers over her cheek. She startles in surprise and I withdraw, but she grasps my hand and puts it back on her cheek.

"Drew," she murmurs, and I kiss her.

I slant my lips and press a single kiss to hers, wait for a beat, and then I kiss her again. She kisses me back, and then we both withdraw, our faces a couple inches apart.

"You have an unfortunate taste in dessert," I say, "but otherwise…"

"No, I think you're the one with unfortunate taste in dessert. Everybody loves ice cream, except you."

She slides the spoon into her mouth and eats the matcha cheesecake ice cream that was meant for me. Then she cups my face in her hands. She's so gentle. I'm not used to anyone being gentle with me, and I like it. I do. But I'm desperate to feel more of her, so I grab her ass and pull her onto my lap.

This kiss is needy with our desperation to get closer and closer. And yes, her lips are a little cold from the ice cream, but just for a moment before they capture my warmth.

It feels wonderful to have a woman in my lap, to have *Chloe* in my lap. I run my hands through her hair, which is a rich, dark brown, and press her closer to me. I want to feel all of her.

She does taste faintly of matcha and cream, but that's only a small part of her taste. In fact, she tastes so fucking amazing, even better than bourbon barrel-aged imperial stout and chocolate, which is my gold standard. Even better than ice cream did back when I was young.

She presses her chest against mine and tightens her thighs around my hips.

God, I want her.

I want to trail kisses down her naked body and listen to her sighs of pleasure. I want to suck on her nipples. I want my head between her legs. I want to brush my cock against her slit and hear her beg.

I want all that. Badly.

But it's not that simple.

I've had sex a few times in the past three years, but not many. All of those times, we met at a bar, and it was obvious from the beginning that a one-night stand was what was on the table. We would fuck and go our separate ways. It would be purely sexual.

Right now... Oh, it's sexual, of course it is. I'm hardening against her, and there's no way she could miss that.

But it's not only sexual.

As I hold her, it's filling some other kind of need inside me. I hadn't realized that I missed simply being close to someone, physically, until now, but apparently I did.

Should I ask if she wants to come home with me?

I don't know.

I don't know anything anymore.

I'm lost.

We separate, ever so slightly, and she tucks a lock of hair behind her ear and looks down shyly—she's never seemed like a shy woman to me before, but there it is. Perhaps she's in desperate need of human touch, too.

Which makes me angry. Chloe should not be starved for physical affection.

I wrap her hair around my hand, and she tentatively slides her hands under my shirt.

"Is this okay?" she asks.

I nod.

She explores my stomach and chest with her fingers, her breath in time with mine.

Maybe if she'd read chapter three of *Embrace Your Inner Ice*

Cream Sandwich, she wouldn't be here on my lap. Maybe this will be the only chance I have to go to bed with her.

I think she'd come home with me now, if I asked.

I don't ask.

Because one night of sex, with me worried she'll lose interest the minute she reads that chapter, doesn't appeal. I'm not sure what I want, however. I don't do things like kiss girls in empty ice cream shops anymore.

I need some time to figure it out.

I press my lips against hers and feast on her mouth again, drowning out my thoughts for a few precious moments. Her hands climb further up my chest, and she circles a fingertip over my nipple, making me gasp.

She smiles, the smile of a woman who knows how much power she has.

"Has it been a long time since you were with a guy?" I push up the bottom of her shirt and idly drag my hand across her bare skin.

She looks at me, as though considering her answer.

"It's none of my business," I say quickly. "You don't need to answer."

"I'll answer." She pauses. "Yes, it's been a while, but...I'm bi. The last time I was with a woman—that was more recent."

My hands still on her stomach, just for a second, and then I nod.

I want to know everything about her. Does she have siblings? A pink flamingo umbrella? How does it feel to be inside her?

I have a feeling my imagination isn't quite good enough for that.

Everything I learn about her is magnificent.

"Is my streak going to end tonight?" she asks.

I shake my head. "No."

"Dammit," she mutters, and I laugh.

I slide my mouth up her neck, to her ear. "Soon, I hope."

But it's getting late and I've had enough confusing thoughts for today. I pick her up and set her feet on the floor. Her hair is a little mussed now, and her lips are slightly swollen from our kisses. I want to see what she looks like when she's even more disheveled, when she's been well fucked. We would be good together in bed. That, I know, even if I don't know much else.

"Goodnight," I say, bending down to kiss her on the cheek. I brush my lips over her temple and whisper, "I'm going to think about you in the shower tonight."

I hear her sharp intake of breath as I head out the door and into the light rain.

[10]
CHLOE

THERE'S no way I'll be able to sleep tonight without getting myself off first.

Not after Drew kissed me.

Not after he held me close, his erection between my thighs.

Not after he had the nerve to tease me after saying goodnight. That bastard.

I lie naked in bed, on my back, and I picture Drew in the shower, soapy water streaming down his gorgeous body. I didn't see much of it, but I pressed myself all over him, and I very much liked what I could feel. I picture him taking his cock in hand. It's already a little hard, but as he jacks himself off slowly, it gets longer, harder, and he tilts his head back, under the stream of water.

I grab my dildo—the larger one—out of my night table and slide the tip over my folds. I'm wet for him, I'm ready to take him, but I run the toy over my slit a few more times before I satisfy my urge to be filled. I groan as I push it inside me, imagining it's him, and that I can feel the weight of him on top of me.

Next, I grab my vibrator, the one I bought because it's super quiet, and press it to my clit as I knead my breasts with my other hand.

I tweak my nipple and wish I could feel his mouth there.

Maybe one day.

God, I hope so.

I imagine him in the shower once more, bracing himself against the tile wall with one arm—because the thought of me makes his legs weak—as he touches himself with his other hand, moving faster and faster as he thinks of me grinding myself against him. And then he comes in his hand with a growl.

I set aside the vibrator and turn onto my stomach. I roll my hips against the bed, and I cover my mouth to stifle my moan as the dildo shifts inside me.

What if I were in the shower with him? I could drop to my knees and take his cock between my lips, reveling in his reaction to my mouth…

I roll onto my side and press the vibrator on my clit once more. Tension builds inside me, and my toes curl before my release shatters me.

~

"Chloe?" Valerie says as she opens the door to the back room.

"Uh, yes?"

"I think you should come out front. Drew's here."

I've been hiding in the back, pretending to go over bills, because I'm not sure I can look at Drew without my face turning as red as a tomato.

"Chloe?" Valerie says again. "He's your guy, not mine."

"Either of us can serve any customer," I snap. "He's not *mine.*"

Valerie tilts her head. "Did something happen? Have you seen him since he came to get those pints of ice cream?"

"He came here last night," I say morosely, because I know she won't give this up.

"And that was a bad thing?"

"We kissed, okay?"

"Ooh, now we're getting somewhere."

I say nothing more, just stalk out to the front, where I see Drew and Michelle standing at the counter.

"What can I get you two today?" I focus on Michelle, who smiles up at me.

"I want to try the durian. Please."

"You know what durian is?"

"It's the big spiky fruit in Chinatown!"

"That's right. But it smells bad. Very bad."

"Like stinky cheese! I love stinky cheese. I'm not scared of it."

Oh, man. She's adorable. I look at Drew, and my heart catches in my chest. He's looking at his niece, but then his gaze snaps up to me, and my breathing becomes unsteady.

What were we talking about again?

Durian. Right.

"It's much worse than stinky cheese," I say, "at least any stinky cheese that I've ever had. It's banned on the transit system in Singapore."

She still doesn't seem put off, so I scoop her a small amount of durian ice cream. To be honest, I don't love durian, but Valerie does, and she insisted I make this flavor.

Michelle puts the spoon up to her nose. "It smells like a gas station. How can food smell like that?" Then she puts the spoon in her mouth. "Mm."

"You like it?" I ask.

"Yeah, but not as much as the other flavors."

"Thank God," Drew mutters.

"I will get ginger and taro," Michelle says. "Please."

"And I'll get a coffee," Drew says. "Plus I'll pay for the tea, too."

It takes me a moment to realize what he's talking about, and then my face heats as I remember last night. As I remember sitting on his lap and feeling up his chest.

And later, making myself come while I thought of him.

"Um. No. That's okay. On the house."

"I insist," he says, so I ring it up because I'm not up to arguing right now.

Once they have their coffee and ice cream, they go to sit by the rocking unicorn. I serve the next customers in line, though I keep stealing glances at Drew. He's wearing jeans and a polo shirt today. The shirt is loose—it's not the optimal piece of clothing for displaying his muscles, but I have a good imagination and I know how he feels, even if I've never seen him shirtless.

When I've finished serving the customers in line, Drew walks over. "Come sit with me."

I swallow. "Last time I did that…what we did…would not be appropriate."

The corner of his mouth quirks up. "That's true."

"But…" The pull he has on me is too strong, and since there are no more customers, I head out from behind the counter. He motions me to the table next to the one where Michelle is sitting. She's finished her ice cream, and he pulls out a box. "Remember how I said we would stay here a little longer today, and you could color?"

She nods, and he puts a sheet of paper in front of her and takes out a package of crayons.

"I'll be right here beside you, talking to Chloe."

"You're talking about adult things?"

"Yes."

"Food isn't an adult thing."

He looks like he's suppressing a smile. "Don't worry, Michelle. We won't talk about food without you."

He sits across from me, coffee in hand. "So."

"So," I say.

He scratches the back of his neck, and oh my God, I find it adorable that he's not some smooth, charming guy who always knows exactly what to say.

"The coffee is good," he says at last.

"The Vietnamese coffee ice cream is good, too," I counter.

He chuckles while still retaining his scowl.

"Or you could try our pie à la mode special. Coconut pie and green tea ice cream."

"You know I don't eat ice cream."

"You know I'm determined to change your mind."

"I know," he says. "What are your, uh, plans for the rest of the weekend?"

"I work on the weekends. It's when we're busiest."

"Right. Of course."

"On Sunday night, I sometimes… Oh, shit. Tomorrow is my mother's birthday." I don't know how I forgot. "She would have been fifty-six."

He squeezes my hand under the table. Just a simple squeeze, but it's more meaningful than it should be.

Neither of us speaks for a minute, and then he says, "Would you like to go out tomorrow morning, before Ginger Scoops opens? We could have brunch."

I don't understand. Is he asking me on a date?

"So you don't have to be alone tomorrow," he clarifies.

Okay. Not a date, but it sounds lovely.

"Sure."

"Do you know any brunch restaurants in the area?" he asks. "Because I confess, brunch isn't something I've done in a long, long time."

"Um…" I can't think of anything, either.

"Or we could have dumplings in Chinatown? I know a place."

"That sounds perfect."

"What's your number? I'll text you later with the address and we'll figure out the time."

Before I can reply, Michelle comes over to our table.

"You said you wouldn't talk about food." She jabs a finger in

Drew's direction. "But you were talking about ice cream. And dumplings."

Drew laughs, then follows Michelle back to her table. I glance over and see that she's drawn a large bowl of ice cream. She asks her uncle how to spell "ice cream sundae" and writes it down.

Seeing Drew and Michelle together causes something to knot in my chest. I picture him with his own children—with *our* children—and then I shake my head.

I am getting way, way ahead of myself.

And I remind myself that he was left at the altar and skewered in a bestselling book—he's probably not interested in anything serious. Plus, I haven't been able to have a proper relationship since my mom died. I've felt too disconnected from people I'm supposed to be intimate with; I haven't been able to truly invest myself in any relationship.

I always feel like I don't quite belong. Although last night, when I was in his lap, pressed against him, I did feel like I was fully there. Whereas with other people I've kissed, there's been a sort of distance, despite the physical contact.

I don't know. I'm probably reading too much into this.

We had one make-out session. So what?

And tomorrow? It's just dumplings.

Dumplings, nothing more.

It's just dumplings, I tell myself as I enter the restaurant.

There are no other customers here. It's two minutes after eleven and they just opened, so that's not surprising. A woman comes over to me, regards me for a moment, and starts speaking in Mandarin. I catch a word or two, but nothing more. Before I can say anything, she switches to English and tells me to sit wherever I like. After I take a seat in the middle of the restaurant, she brings over a teapot and a teacup.

"I'm waiting for someone," I say.

She nods and brings another teacup.

Drew is only four minutes late now, but I can't help worrying that he won't show up and I'll be stuck here eating dumplings alone, feeling like I don't belong. Although I want dumplings, perhaps this wasn't the greatest idea—I feel "other" in China-town, just like I feel "other" when I'm with my father's family.

I don't speak Cantonese or Mandarin, aside from the little I learned when I took that class. I can't read the language. I don't look quite right. I've never been to China.

I don't share a lot of experiences that other people of Chinese descent share.

I don't even have any Asian relatives anymore.

I feel like a fraud.

Well, that's not quite true about the relatives. There's Aunt Anita in New York City, but I haven't seen her in ages. I feel like she's abandoned me, though I shouldn't feel that way.

I pour myself some tea, then start to read the menu to calm my mind. Each item is listed both in Chinese and English and has a number beside it. There are little sheets of paper and pencils for you to write down the number corresponding to each of the dishes you want.

Okay. I'll read the menu over slowly, and if Drew still isn't here by the time I've finished, I'll order something. This will be fine, even if I have to do it alone.

I'm on the "boiled dumpling" section of the menu when Drew walks in, and I want to weep in relief, which is ridiculous. He comes to sit across from me.

I pour him some tea, my hand shaking on the teapot.

"Are you okay, Chloe?" he asks, taking the teapot from me.

"I'm fine."

He tilts his head in an I-don't-believe-you manner. "I'm sorry I'm late."

"You were less than ten minutes late." I try to be reasonable. "It's no big deal."

He touches my knee under the table. "Do you know what you want to eat?"

"Um." Suddenly, figuring that out seems like an insurmountable problem.

"I'll order for us," he says. "If that's okay. Is there anything you can't have?"

I shake my head.

He removes his hand from my knee and picks up the menu, but his other hand closes around mine on top of the table. This small gesture feels like a very public declaration.

I like it.

The server comes over to our table. Drew hands the paper to her and says a few words in English, and then his attention is on me. His expression is serious but kind.

I feel like I could say anything, and he would listen, and it would be okay.

"My mom loved her birthday," I say, "and she never tried to hide her age. When she turned fifty, she said the whole year would be a celebration."

He smiles faintly and rubs his thumb over my hand.

I take a deep breath, and then I tell him something I've never told anyone else. "Ice cream makes me happy, but really, the ice cream shop is for her. In her memory. I decided I would have Asian flavors, because my mom was Asian, and God, it sounds stupid when I put it like that, but as soon as I thought of it, I loved the idea. Green tea and red bean and coconut…"

"And durian."

"Yes. But that's only because Valerie insisted." I pause. "Since my mom died, I've felt like half of me has been wiped from existence. Like more than just my mother is gone. But reading Chinese history and folklore and trying to learn a language she never spoke didn't help me feel more connected."

He doesn't speak; he just listens and continues to stroke my hand.

"I needed something else, so now I make green tea and ginger ice cream, in an ice cream shop just outside of Chinatown." I shrug. "It feels so frivolous, to have an ice cream shop in my mother's memory. An *ice cream* shop."

"It's not frivolous," he says.

Which is the first time anyone has ever said that to me, but I've never given anyone the chance to say it to me before; I don't talk about this, not even with Valerie.

"I'm a frivolous woman," I insist. "I have an ice cream shop with pink walls and rainbows and unicorns, and I wear a frilly apron because I like it. I was planning to go to dental school, but then my mom died and I quit university. You think I'm ridiculous, don't you? You, who doesn't even like ice cream."

"Chloe, I don't think you're ridiculous. I think you should do what makes you happy—"

"Do you?"

"—in a sensible way," he finishes. "I assume you have a solid business plan?"

"Why do you think that?"

He shrugs. "Because I don't think you're frivolous and ridiculous. You just have very different, uh, tastes than I do."

"My dad thinks I'm ridiculous. And he said he didn't think of my mother as Chinese, and he's confused by all my Asian ice cream flavors. I'm his, so I must be white. Or he thinks of me as colorless, because he believes it's best not to see color."

I'm rambling. I don't know what I'm doing. I just have all these thoughts crowding my brain, and they're popping out at random, even though I usually keep these things to myself. But for once, I'm not filtering what I'm saying.

Why with Drew? Why not with Valerie? Or Lillian?

"My white relatives are nice," I say, "but I feel a little removed from them. They're family, though. I shouldn't feel that way. Outside of my family, it feels like white people think of me as Asian, and Asian people think of me as white—nobody sees me as one of their own. Like here." I gesture around the room. "I don't belong."

He squeezes my hand again, as though saying, *You do*.

I close my eyes for a moment, concentrating on his hand on mine, before I continue.

"Asian people are expected to be either immigrants or the children of immigrants. If we're raised here, we're supposed to be struggling with the divide with our parents, who were raised in a different country. But I'm third generation, not second generation. Unlike the kids I went to school with. Unlike the Asian Americans in the TV shows I watch."

"I know how you feel."

I manage a smile. It's rare for someone to say that to me. "What was it like for you?"

"I told you my father was born here, right?" he says, and I nod. "It always surprises people when I say that. My mother didn't grow up here, though, and I think that's a lot of the reason why my parents had different ideas on how we should be raised. They fought about it quite a bit."

A bamboo steamer is set in front of us. Drew opens it up to reveal twelve dumplings.

"I think these are the beef and celery," he says.

I reach for a dumpling with my chopsticks and pop it in my mouth. It's a little too hot, but it's tasty.

We eat in silence for a few minutes. I feel like I need the silence after what I said. It's weird to talk about things like this.

My mom died, and I miss her. But the effects of her death rippled through my life, affecting what I do for work, how I feel about myself, and how I relate to my father—and people in general.

What would it be like if she'd lived?

I want that so desperately. I'd be a different person. I don't know who.

Drew hasn't lost a parent, and he isn't biracial. He doesn't have exactly the same family history as me, but there are similarities. More than with most people.

And I just like talking to him.

I don't know what it is about him, because it's not his frown or his really great arms—though they are quite fine—or the quiet concentration in his expression.

"Have you been to China?" I ask.

"I've been to Hong Kong several times to visit my mom's family. I've also been to Beijing, and I've seen the Great Wall."

"Have you been to where your father's family is from?"

He shakes his head.

I can't help my disappointment. I was so hoping he'd been. I'm curious.

"My paternal grandparents never went back," he says. "They didn't leave under great circumstances, and they never wanted to return. They had no family to visit there—everyone was either dead, or they'd come to North America."

"My grandparents never went back, either. I didn't understand it when I was younger. In every word they spoke, I could hear that they hadn't been raised here, but they rarely talked about the past and never expressed interest in going back. I suppose it would be a completely different place today."

"My parents are in Hong Kong right now."

"For how long?"

"More than a month. It's the longest they've ever stayed, but they're retired and my grandma isn't in great health. It's awkward for my dad because everyone speaks to him in Cantonese, and he doesn't understand the language very well."

The server brings us some pan-fried dumplings.

"Pork and chive," Drew says.

"Ooh, these are my favorite."

I appreciate that he picked out the restaurant and ordered for us. I like not having to make decisions for a day.

And I feel like someone sees me, really sees me.

It's nice.

The server sets another bamboo steamer on our table.

"How much did you order?" I ask Drew.

"This is all, but we can get more if you like."

Suddenly, I'm ravenous. "Maybe we could have more of the pork and chive ones."

Drew asks the server to bring us another order of dumplings before turning back to me. "When do you have to be at Ginger Scoops?"

"Valerie is opening today, but I told her I'd be there by one. I hope it'll be busy. The weather is nice." I nod toward the window.

We chat a little more as we eat. I ask Drew about his job. He's one of those smart finance people who works at a bank on Bay Street. That's something I could never do. Neither my old self—who wanted to be a dentist—nor my new self would do something like that.

By the time we leave, I've eaten twenty-four dumplings.

Hardly a healthy meal, but I feel content.

~

Drew walks me back to Ginger Scoops and comes inside with me.

"How about I get you some ice cream?" I say. "On the house. What would you like—Vietnamese coffee? Chocolate-raspberry? Or maybe you'd fancy some durian? Perhaps some taro? Maybe all four? Usually there are two flavors in a bubble waffle, but I could make a special one for you. And did you know we have rainbow sprinkles and chocolate shavings?"

I can't resist teasing him.

He glares at me, but it's an affectionate glare. "I'm not getting a bubble waffle with four types of ice cream and goddamn rainbow sprinkles."

"Shh. This is a family establishment. No swearing." Although there's only one teenage couple in the shop, and they're making out.

"It's a family establishment?" He raises his eyebrows. "That's news to me."

"You bring your niece here every Saturday."

"Mm-hmm." He pulls me around the corner to the short hallway that leads to the washroom. "But you remember what happened on Friday night?"

My cheeks heat. "I do."

We're separate from the rest of the shop now, leaning against the bright pink wall. He rubs his thumb over my chin. "I seem to recall you sitting in my lap and pressing yourself all over me."

"Why wouldn't you take me home with you?"

"Chloe." He runs his hand through my hair. "Let me take you out next weekend. On a proper date. Saturday?"

I very much want that. In fact, I want to wrap my arms tightly around him and keep him with me all day, but I have a business to run. Saturday will have to do.

"I'll be working until after nine, so it'll have to be a late date."

"No problem." He winks at me before he heads out.

Six days until I see him again.

I can't wait.

WHEN I GET home from Ginger Scoops, I head to the balcony with a beer, some chocolate, and a book. Having finished *Embrace Your Inner Ice Cream Sandwich*, I'm now cleansing my palate with a thriller. I bought one that sounded particularly dark, horrific, and gruesome.

It should be the perfect thing to help me forget about ice cream and oatmeal cookies with raisins. Bleh.

Hopefully it'll also be the perfect thing to help me forget about the truly bizarre dream I had last night. I'd call it a nightmare, except I'm hesitant to call anything with unicorns a nightmare.

In my dream, I was at Michelle's birthday party, but I was Tinker Bell-sized and invisible to humans. When the girls went to the dining room to have cake and ice cream, the unicorn figurines came to life and started chasing me. The Goth unicorn was particularly ferocious, though the one covered in glitter was a close second. I soon discovered that painting a heart on every unicorn's ass was a giant mistake, as apparently they could shoot ice cream sandwiches out of their heart tattoos. So there I was, running around the house, being chased by unicorns that were shooting ice cream and cookies out of their asses.

It was fucking terrifying.

Is that dream supposed to mean something? I don't think so. But it's by far the most disturbing dream I've had in years.

And if you're wondering how it ended? Well, Goth Unicorn and Glitter Unicorn cornered me under the table, and they had the most vicious expressions on their faces, and then...

I woke up.

I know, I know, it wasn't a very satisfying ending.

My life has been so strange lately. I've somehow managed to find myself at a paint-your-own-unicorn children's party and the most disgustingly-cute gift store in existence. I've also been frequenting an ice cream parlor.

And I asked a woman out today.

I hadn't done that in years, not since I met Lisa.

I wasn't sure I'd ever be able to do this again. I mean, given that I was left at the altar and had the details of that relationship read by millions of people in twenty-three languages, I'm a little damaged. That's reasonable, isn't it?

But Chloe makes me want to try again, though I'm not thinking too much about where this is going. I just know that I want to spend time with her.

I appreciate that she's unabashed in what she likes. I appreciate her fucking sunshine personality, even if she makes me want to roll my eyes at times.

Yet I also want to be there when she isn't all sunshine and rainbows. I want to be there when she's thinking about her mom and when she's talking about how she doesn't belong anywhere. Earlier, I nearly pulled her into my arms and said something really cheesy. *You belong with me.*

Like I said, really cheesy.

My heart fucking aches at the thought that this woman, who's so loving and giving, doesn't get enough affection and feels removed from the world around her.

I know what that feels like.

Because even though I'm a grumpy bastard who stomps all over people's dreams, sometimes I just want a cuddle, you know?

Cuddling is pretty awesome, not that I would ever admit that to anyone.

I don't know what it's like to lose a parent. I haven't experienced a lot of the things she's gone through. But like Chloe, I do feel a bit removed from everything around me, ever since I was left at the altar. We're a little alike, except it makes perfect sense for me to be alone in the world, whereas it doesn't make sense for her.

I sip my beer and open my book, but I can't concentrate on murders and blood, not now. I can't help thinking about where I should take her on Saturday.

I also can't help thinking about what she'll wear, and how it'll feel to undress her.

Because I totally plan on doing that, if she's interested.

As it turns out, I can't wait until Saturday.

Wednesday after work, I start walking home from the office, but I'm hit with an overwhelming need to see Chloe Jenkins. So instead, I go to Baldwin Village, my heart beating faster as I approach Ginger Scoops.

Unfortunately, there's a large group of teenage girls inside, and their orders contain lots of bubble waffles and various toppings. I wait impatiently behind them. Chloe notices me and shoots me a smile, and something inside me practically soars, just at her smile. Almost like someone dumped a bowl of glitter on me.

Disturbing.

At last, I'm at the front of the line.

"It's nice to see a regular," she says in her customer service voice. "You always order the same thing. Let me see if I can remember—it's quite a complicated order." She pauses dramatically. "Ah, yes. A bubble waffle with Vietnamese coffee, chocolate-raspberry, durian, and taro?"

I give her a dark look.

"You're right," she says. "Can't forget about the rainbow sprinkles."

"Mommy!" says the little boy in line behind me. "That sounds amazing. Can I order it?"

Chloe laughs and hands her ice cream scoop over to Valerie. There's no one else in line behind me except the little boy, his mother, and his baby sister.

"Come with me." Chloe grabs my hand and leads me into a storage room, and as soon as the door is closed, she presses me against it, stands on her toes, and kisses me like we haven't seen each other in a year.

I can't remember the last time anyone was so excited to see me.

"God, you look hot," she says, finally tearing her lips away, leaving me panting.

"You like the corporate look?" I gesture to my blue dress shirt and tie. "I wasn't sure it would be your thing."

"You pull it off well." She grins up at me.

I make her smile like this. Me, Drew Lum. Aka Marvin Wong, terrible boyfriend extraordinaire, known for melting people's ice cream sandwiches and stifling creative energy.

But I want Chloe to have everything. I want her to make as much Vietnamese coffee ice cream and strawberry-lychee sorbet and bubble waffles as she likes, even if they're not my cup of tea.

I want her to feel like she belongs.

I wrap my arms around her and pull her close, and then I crush my lips against hers as I slide my hands down her back to cup her ass. She melts against me, and God, it's glorious to have her in my arms like this. Her tongue slips into my mouth and touches mine, and I groan, a groan that only intensifies as she arches against me.

Fuck, I want her.

I was going to wait until Saturday, but I have a condom with me, and while the storage room in the back of an ice cream parlor isn't ideal...

"How long do you have?" I murmur.

"Not long enough."

"Dammit."

She jumps up and wraps her legs around my waist, and we kiss frantically. Her mouth is perfect on mine. I didn't think it was possible, but now I want her even more, the waves of desire nearly consuming me. I need to be closer to her. Within her. Learning every inch of her body and making her come on my cock.

And then she slides down and her feet touch the floor. To my satisfaction, her pupils are dilated and her cheeks are an attractive pink hue, but she's not touching me anymore and I can barely stand it. I *ache* for her.

"You're beautiful," I breathe, my fingers trailing over her flushed skin.

"Saturday," she says. "Saturday."

I helplessly follow her back into the shop.

I can't get that kiss out of my mind all evening.

Finally, it's Saturday. My last day of looking after Michelle, and my first proper date with Chloe. Hopefully it'll also be the first time I have sex in over a year, but I try not to think about that while my niece is sitting in my living room with me. She's asking me spelling questions about cheese.

"How do you spell Gorgonzola, Uncle Drew?"

"G-O-R-G-O-N-Z-O-L-A."

Michelle is almost finished kindergarten now. She knows her letters, but she can't read very well. As she writes the letters with utmost concentration, her tongue sticking out of the side of her mouth, I feel a strange pressure in my chest.

Lisa knew I wanted kids, then wrote some not-so-flattering words about me being a dad.

I push those memories aside.

I've enjoyed spending time with Michelle in the past month. I hadn't spent a great deal of time with my niece before, except at family get-togethers. When she was a baby, I was afraid I would break her, and I didn't know how to interact with someone who couldn't speak. And then when she was a little older, there was that ice cream truck experience.

But now, we get along pretty well.

I left my unicorn figurine at Michelle's house, but she brought it with her today and insisted I keep it. She's named it Havarti Sparkles—she's on a bit of a cheese kick today. Havarti Sparkles is currently sitting on the table, regarding Michelle as she writes her list of cheese, complete with illustrations. Although to be honest, every picture she draws of cheese looks the same to me.

"Cheddar?" She looks up at me.

"C-H-E-D-D-A-R."

She carefully writes that on the paper. "Mozzarella?"

Uh-oh. I'm not sure about that one. It's not like knowing how to spell "mozzarella" is relevant to my career in finance. Plus, you know, there's this thing called spellcheck.

"M-O-Z-Z-E-R-E-L-L-A," I tell Michelle, hoping it's right.

I surreptitiously look it up on my phone and discover my error. Oops.

"Brie?"

"B-R-I-E."

By the time she's finished her list, it has twelve cheeses. I'm impressed she knows that many.

"Let's go out for lunch now," I say. "You still want to try the Korean-Polish place?"

"Yes! Can Havarti Sparkles come with us?" She looks up at me with serious eyes, and then she puts her hands together, pleading with me.

Oh, fuck. I can't say no to her.

"Um, okay." I scratch the back of my neck. "You can bring Havarti Sparkles."

"I'll put her in my purse!"

Of course, by the time we're a block from my condo, Michelle has tired of carrying her purse, so when we enter the restaurant, I'm the one carrying the pink Hello Kitty purse that contains a unicorn figurine.

Two hours later, we're sitting in Ginger Scoops, Michelle eating her ice cream—black sesame and passionfruit—under the watchful eye of Havarti Sparkles. Frankly, after my dream last week, that unicorn is creeping me out. I keep imagining her shooting giant ice cream sandwiches out of her ass.

I'm a normal guy, clearly.

My gaze drifts toward the counter, where Chloe and Valerie are serving a large family. Chloe is wearing a reddish shirt and jeans, plus an apron. I wonder if that's what she'll wear tonight, or whether she'll change. I assume she'll take off the apron, though I rather like it. It's white with ruffles, some embroidered flowers on the bottom.

It would look very nice with nothing on underneath, though that would be inappropriate attire for the place I'm going to take her tonight.

I like spending the day with Michelle, but my God, I can't wait until this evening.

When there are no more customers to serve, Chloe comes over to our table.

"Did you enjoy your ice cream?" she asks Michelle.

Michelle nods. "It was very tasty, thank you."

"Who's this?" Chloe taps the unicorn on the table.

"That's Havarti Sparkles!"

Chloe laughs—she has such a nice laugh. Just the sound of her laugh makes the corners of my mouth twitch, and frankly, it's usually difficult to coax a smile out of me.

"Havarti is a cheese," Michelle explains. "Do you think unicorns like cheese?"

"Well, I don't see how anyone could dislike cheese."

Michelle nods again, as though this is only sensible.

"Would you like to color?" I take the crayons and hedgehog notepad out of her purse, and Michelle gets to work. I'm not sure what she's drawing, but it's red and green and pink.

Once Michelle is distracted, I turn back to Chloe and slide my hand up her leg.

"Are you ready for tonight?" I murmur.

"Very. Where are you taking me for our date?"

"Date?" Michelle shrieks. "You're going on a date? With Uncle Drew? Chloe and Drew, sitting in a tree. K-I-S-S-I-N-G. First comes love, then comes—"

"Michelle." I grit my teeth. "You're too loud. You're disturbing the other people."

She continues at a marginally quieter volume. "First comes love, then comes marriage, then comes the baby in the baby carriage. I can't wait to tell Mommy!"

No, no, no.

"Don't tell your mother that I'm going on a date."

"Why not? She'll be happy you have a girlfriend!"

"Chloe isn't my girlfriend."

Michelle frowns. "If you're going on a date, doesn't that mean she's your girlfriend?"

"It's not that simple."

"I don't understand adults."

"Please don't say anything."

"Why not?"

I sigh. "If you promise not to tell your mother, I'll buy you another ice cream right now."

Michelle's eyes go wide. "Really? A second ice cream?"

"Any flavors you like."

"Durian and green tea, please," she says to Chloe.

Yeah, this is fucking perfect. I just bribed a six-year-old with ice cream, and after two servings, she's probably going to be hyper, and there's still no guarantee she won't tell Adrienne. Plus she asked for durian ice cream, so now the table is going to smell like natural gas.

Yeah. Just fucking great.

But then I look at Chloe, returning to the table with a little cup of ice cream, and when she smiles at me, I feel like the luckiest guy in the world.

[13]

CHLOE

DREW and I are sitting side-by-side in a small-plates restaurant just off College Street. The bartender pours my pink drink into a glass with a flourish and garnishes it with a skewer of raspberries. Then he makes Drew's less colorful drink.

It's a Southeast Asian fusion place in an old, narrow house. The lights are dim; the décor is eclectic. It has a quirky, intimate feel.

Not that it matters much. We could be at a Taco Bell right now and I would still be bouncing in my seat, as long as he was sitting next to me.

Drew is wearing a black button-down shirt and dark jeans, and he looks pretty hot. Me, on the other hand? I'm wearing the same thing I put on this morning: jeans and the burgundy shirt that my friends said did great things for my boobs. I thought I looked cute earlier, but now, I fear I look a little ragged.

But when I run my hand up Drew's thigh, he inhales sharply.

I used to be good at this stuff. I dated a lot in university, and it was fun. Tonight, however, I find myself second-guessing everything, and I have no idea what to say. I've already told him lots of things, some of which I've never told anyone else.

I really want this to go well.

Just relax. It's Drew. Everything will be okay.

The music is a mix of hits from the seventies, eighties, and nineties, and the piña colada song comes on. When I giggle, he turns to me and raises an eyebrow.

"I'm picturing you drinking a piña colada," I say, "with a pineapple garnish and a little umbrella."

"Oh, the horror," he mutters.

I wrap my arm around him and sing along for a few lines. "You seem a bit tense."

"I haven't been on a date in a long time."

"Same here."

I pull back, and we look at each other, really look at each other in the dim light of the restaurant. When I start singing again, he gives me a hint of a smile. Or perhaps that's my imagination. There are a couple candles on the bar, and shadows flicker over his face.

"I take it you don't sing," I say.

He shakes his head.

"Or dance."

"That would be a no."

"Or write poetry?

"As if."

"But here's something you do." I lower my voice and shift my stool closer to his so I can press up against his arm. "You think of me when you're in the shower."

And now, I have completely shifted the mood.

"I told you I would do that," he says, a little hoarsely.

"Sometimes, I think you jerk off when you think of me in the shower."

"Christ, Chloe."

Tonight, I want the physical intimacy that we both crave. I'm determined to make him want me more than he's ever wanted anyone. I want to seduce him, but I don't simply want to seduce him for the physical act of sex; I need it to be more than just a fuck, and I think he needs it, too.

I lean in again. With the music and the chatter around us, if I whisper in his ear, no one will hear. "I want to know if you got yourself off that night in the shower. I thought of you doing it, you know."

Lately, this hasn't been me. I've gone after some things I want —like the ice cream shop—but I haven't been brave with people. I haven't told my friends and family what I'm really thinking, and I haven't gone after people I want romantically.

Though I hadn't wanted anyone for a long time before I met Drew.

I take a deep breath. "I went home, and I made myself come as I pictured you alone in the shower, fisting your cock, soapy water cascading over your skin."

"Fuck," he says, as though he's in physical pain.

As though hearing me talk like this is too much for him to bear.

"So," I say casually, "did you think of me and jerk off while I was thinking of you?"

"Yes." His voice is clipped, but his warm breath caresses my cheek. "You know I did."

I shift awkwardly in my seat, my pulse throbbing between my legs, and just as I'm about to speak again, a plate of mango salad with skewers of shrimp is set in front of us.

Right. Food.

We stumble into his apartment after midnight, and as soon as the door closes, he flicks on the lights and pushes me against the wall. His mouth is on mine immediately, greedy and insistent, and I know right away that I've lost all control of the situation. I may have been the one in control at the restaurant, but now, the tables have turned.

"You were driving me mad at dinner," he says. "Such a naughty girl, telling me you touched yourself, when I couldn't do anything about the moisture pooling between your legs."

I shiver in anticipation.

"Is this okay?" he whispers, his voice gentle now. "If I talk like this?"

He'll give me the control back, if I want it, which makes me want to give it to him even more.

When I nod, he kisses the side of my neck and undoes the bow at the side of my wrap shirt, sliding it off my shoulders. It falls to the floor, a pool by my feet.

"But now we're alone." His gaze is molten, but his words are calm, measured, commanding. "Get naked."

A part of me wants to be contrary, but I do as he asks.

"Sit on the coffee table." He points behind me. "Spread your legs."

"Do you get off on being bossy?"

"Maybe just a little."

I figured he wouldn't be much of a talker in the bedroom, but I was wrong. So wrong.

I sit on the coffee table and spread my legs, as requested. I feel vulnerable. It's almost too much, but I force myself to keep still, to keep my knees apart, and I look up at Drew.

His eyes are smoldering as he stalks toward me. "Very nice."

I tell myself to keep breathing.

"You're fucking gorgeous, Chloe."

"Thank you."

"I can't wait to pull one of your pretty nipples between my teeth and bury my face between your legs."

"Drew…"

"But first." He puts his hands on his hips. "Show me how you touched yourself when you thought of me."

"You're evil." I'm desperate for his touch, but he won't give it to me.

He smirks. "Maybe a little. You're not the first person to say that."

"I can't do it, though. I was using toys, and I don't have them here."

"Why did we go to my place instead of yours?"

"Because I live in a house with three grad students and only have a twin bed."

He exhales, and then he unzips his pants. I watch with unbearable anticipation as he pulls out his cock and strokes himself once, from the base to the tip.

I want him so badly.

"This is what I did when I thought of you," he says.

"Except I assume you weren't wearing pants in the shower."

"Details, details. Tell me about these toys. Did you use a vibrator?"

"Of course."

He strokes himself again. "You want to be filled with my cock right now, don't you?"

I reach for him, but he slaps my hand away.

"Not yet," he says.

He's so close to me, and it's torture to see him fisting his cock when I'm not allowed to touch. He's hard, and his skin looks satiny. I'm mesmerized.

Drew's gaze drops from my eyes to between my legs. "You're wet. May I touch you?"

I nod eagerly, and he chuckles. It reverberates through my body.

He kneels between my legs. When his fingers brush over my slit, I gasp. It's been so long since someone has touched me intimately.

"Very wet," he murmurs as he pulls his hand away.

"You can keep going."

"I could. Or…" He takes my hand in his and puts it between my legs. "I want to see you touch yourself."

It feels particularly revealing to do this in his presence. My cheeks heat as I part my folds and slip two fingers inside.

"Yes, baby," he says. "So fucking pretty."

I hold his gaze as I slide my fingers in and out. *Oh, fuck.* This is almost too intense.

I'm fully bare before him, my fingers in my pussy. So sensitive to every touch, every look he gives me.

Vulnerable, yes.

I wouldn't do this with a one-night stand.

"Very nice." He keeps murmuring his appreciation, making it easy to continue. Except…

"You know," I say, "you could do some of the work rather than just kneeling there."

"You have a bit of a mouth on you."

"Why don't you put my mouth to better use?"

The room is quiet for a moment, aside from the sound of my fingers sliding in and out of my wetness, and then he bursts into laughter.

Somehow, that laughter makes the moment even more intimate.

"Very well," he says at last, and then he kisses me on the lips.

I melt against him as he plunders my mouth, and oh God, he tastes good. It's like a feast to have his open mouth against mine, his tongue darting between my lips. One of his hands gently cups my head, and the other slips between my legs and pushes my hand out of the way so he can take over. He slides one long finger inside me, and another massages my clit.

"Drew," I gasp.

He resumes kissing me and pushes another finger inside me. I squirm against him.

"Good?" he murmurs, smiling against my lips.

"Why do you ask such silly questions?"

"It's not a silly question. Your pleasure is very important to me."

"But the answer to the question is obvious."

"Mm. That it is."

I grab his cock, and he jerks up. "I think you should lose some of those clothes. I'm naked and you're not. It's hardly fair."

"As you wish." He stands up and unbuttons his shirt. He tosses it aside, then pushes down his jeans and boxers and steps out of them.

He's glorious.

And judging by the smug look on his face, he knows it.

Perhaps because I'm practically drooling.

Drew kneels between my legs once more and drops his mouth to the junction between them. He gives my slit one long lick. I grip the sides of the coffee table. Then he slips his fingers inside me again and circles his tongue around my clit.

"You know what else you'd be good at?" I say, smirking. "Licking an ice cream cone."

"Not funny. And if you're still able to make smart-ass comments like that, then clearly I'm not doing my job."

He buries his face between my legs and strokes me more insistently.

Oh, fuck. I'm definitely not capable of speech now. I spiral higher and higher, toward that wonderful peak. Every muscle in my body tightens, then releases, and I cry out in ecstasy.

My vibrator never gives me an orgasm quite like *that*.

He licks me slowly through my climax, then gathers my boneless body in his arms and carries me to the bedroom. He deposits me carefully on the bed and climbs on top of me. So much of my skin is against his, and it feels wonderful. I run my hands all over his back, then around to his abs.

"Are you ready to take me?" he asks.

"God, yes."

He rolls on a condom and runs his cock over my slit as he

smooths my hair and looks into my eyes. "I've wanted to do this for a long time."

My heart beats loudly in my chest. I want him. I want him so much.

The tip of his cock presses inside me, and I gasp. Slowly, he slides all the way in.

"How's that?" he whispers.

I nod, unable to speak. He's inside me, on top of me, all around me; I am acutely aware of how close we are.

Drew props himself up on one elbow, and his other hand comes up to my cheek. He begins to move inside me, his gaze intense on my face.

I feel like he can see every inch of me.

And I don't want to hide.

"You feel amazing," I whisper.

"So do you," he says, wonder in his voice.

I pull his head down to mine and kiss him greedily. His mouth and tongue pleasure me as he pushes inside me, then retreats, keeping up a steady rhythm that drives me mad. I arch my hips against him and wrap my legs around his waist.

We move in unison, two people who almost always spend our nights alone. But tonight, we're together, and when our bodies separate, we won't go back to the way we were before.

His thrusts become deeper, and I welcome it. He slides his hand between our bodies and rubs my clit. I explode around him, and he follows me, growling my name as he comes.

When Drew returns from the washroom, I wrap my arms around him and revel in the feeling of having him naked in bed. He runs his hands through my hair and presses himself against me, and God, it's perfect.

"I figured you wouldn't like cuddling," I say.

"Why not?"

"It doesn't fit with your grumpy exterior. Besides, you don't like ice cream, and *everybody* loves ice cream."

He laughs softly. "I like cuddling. I'm just out of practice."

"Me, too."

"Which is wrong. You should have all the cuddles you could ever want."

"I want an awful lot of cuddles. It might be too much for anyone to handle."

"Challenge accepted." He brushes his mouth over mine and kisses me softly.

Everything is right in the world as I drift off to sleep.

It's white with purple hair and a terrifying pointy horn, and it's chasing me through a land of giant desserts. Slices of chocolate cake that are twice as tall as me. A river of strawberry sauce.

And ice cream, of course.

Lots and lots of ice cream. There's even a giant banana split with sprinkles.

But the unicorn keeps on chasing me, and oh my God, it's got friends. They're pink and purple, and they've got heart tattoos on their asses.

I run through puddles of chocolate sauce, trying to go faster and faster, but they're going to catch me, it's inevitable...

I open my eyes.

I'm not longer in some fucked-up mash-up of *My Little Pony* and *Cloudy with a Chance of Meatballs*. No, I'm in my own bed, and there's a woman beside me, peering at me curiously. She puts a hand on my head.

"Are you okay?" Chloe asks. "You were thrashing about. Did you have a nightmare?"

"Um, no. Just a slightly disturbing dream. Nothing serious."

"Having nightmares is nothing to be ashamed of."

She sounds so kind and concerned. Like she's afraid I've experienced real-life trauma and that's why I'm having these dreams. But I just went to a paint-your-own-unicorn party, and the dream wasn't really that bad.

I start kissing my way down her neck. We're both still naked, and I hope we've got time to have more fun before she heads to work. I glance at the alarm clock on my bedside table and gasp.

Havarti Sparkles is right beside my alarm clock, her evil eyes staring at me. Michelle must have decided the unicorn belonged on my bedside table.

"What's wrong?" Chloe asks.

"Um."

"Talk to me."

"I don't know…"

"Drew, please. What happened?"

"Fine," I say in exasperation. "I had a nightmare about Havarti Sparkles chasing me through a field of giant scoops of ice cream."

She puts her hand to her mouth, as though trying not to laugh.

"There were so many unicorns, all chasing me. They were evil; I could see their evil little eyes and twinkling horns. They wanted to shoot ice cream sandwiches out of the hearts on their asses."

"Why on earth do you think they wanted to do that?"

"Because that's what they did in my last dream."

She looks at me incredulously.

Okay, I think I just destroyed my chances of getting laid this morning. I am so out of practice with women.

"Want some breakfast?" I ask, climbing out of bed. I'm a little self-conscious of my nudity now. "We can have cereal, or I can make you some eggs. How do you like your eggs?"

Chloe sits up and the blanket tumbles down her chest, exposing her breasts. They are indeed lovely breasts, and I didn't give them enough attention last night.

I want them in my mouth, but I don't think that's going to happen.

I swallow. "Eggs?"

"Drew, are you okay? You're not shaken up?"

"I'm fine. Just embarrassed."

"Am I allowed to laugh? Because I've never heard of an adult having nightmares about unicorns and ice cream and I can barely..." And there come the giggles.

I just stand there, hands on my hips. Perhaps I would present an imposing figure if I weren't naked and if I hadn't just described my ridiculous nightmare.

"Has it just happened the two times?" she asks.

"Thankfully, yes."

"Come here."

I return to the bed, and she puts her arms around me. Her laughter is contagious, and I start to laugh, too. I look at Havarti Sparkles, sitting imposingly (ha!) on my bedside table, and then at Chloe's lovely face, and I laugh and laugh.

I haven't laughed like this in ages.

Once we've both calmed down, Chloe says, "I know something that will make you forget all about your dream."

"Do you?"

"Mm-hmm."

She scrapes her fingernails down my chest and presses her mouth to mine.

~

As I mop the kitchen floor, I find myself humming the piña colada song. Nothing can get me down right now, not even the mention of ice cream sandwiches.

Chloe left at ten, and I feel like I'm on top of the world. I had a hot woman in my bed last night and this morning, and we made plans to see each other again tonight. Yes, there was the unfortunate bad-dream incident, but it all turned out okay.

The phone rings. It's my mother.

"Drew, can you buzz us in?"

Well, this is unexpected. "Why are you here?"

"I haven't seen you in six weeks. Can't I see my son?"

Hmm. I have a bad feeling about this.

Mom and Dad come up a few minutes later, accompanied by Adrienne and Michelle. Mom gives me a hug and shouts in my ear, "You have a girlfriend and you didn't tell me?"

It turns out that something can get me down after all: my family discussing my love life.

Yeah, this is going to be great. Just great.

"Where did you hear that?" I ask.

"Michelle told me you had a date last night," Adrienne says.

Okay, that's the last time I bribe Michelle. I glare at my niece, then my sister.

"Yes, I had a date, though I don't know why you had to tell Mom and Dad. It was our first date. She's not my girlfriend."

The thought of actually being someone's *boyfriend* still makes me a bit uncomfortable. When I think of what happened with Lisa…

I shake my head to clear it of those thoughts. "How was Hong Kong?"

My parents got back yesterday. Surely they should be at home, recovering from jetlag, rather than interfering in my life.

"Don't change the topic," Mom says. "I hear this woman owns an ice cream shop?"

"She does."

"Ice cream sounds lovely," Dad says. "It's a hot day. Just what I need."

Oh, God. No. He wants to meet Chloe today?

Mom sniffs. "I can't say I approve. Why couldn't you find a doctor or an engineer? Did she go to university?"

"Yes, but she didn't graduate."

Mom's mouth drops open in horror.

"Her mother died while she was in university, and she took some time off. Then she decided she didn't want to go back and would rather do something else with her life."

"I can't believe you, of all people," Adrienne says, "are dating someone who sells ice cream for a living."

"Yeah, well…"

"And I'm the one who made this happen. I told you to take Michelle to Ginger Scoops. I should become a matchmaker!"

"She's so pretty, Po Po," Michelle says to my mother.

"Aiyah! The last one was pretty, too, and look what happened. We wasted so much money."

My parents had insisted on paying for half of the wedding. I told them it was unnecessary, but they refused to listen. I think it was partly because they didn't want Lisa's parents—who are quite well off and could easily have paid for the whole thing—to think they were cheap, then use it as an excuse to say all Chinese people are cheap. Or something like that. I believe it was pride more than anything.

In the unlikely event that I get engaged again, I won't let my parents, or the woman's parents, pay for anything.

Weird that I now see marriage as an unlikely possibility, rather than completely impossible.

"She looks like me!" Michelle grabs my mother's hand.

"Like you?"

"She's mixed race," I say. "Chinese mother, white father. Like Michelle."

"Does she speak Cantonese?" Mom asks hopefully.

"No. Her mother was born here, like Dad, and her family's from Toisan."

"You said her mother was dead?"

I nod.

"Poor girl."

We're all quiet for a moment.

"Well, let's go meet her," Dad says with a mischievous smile. "I could really use some ice cream. Which flavors are good there, Drew?"

"I still haven't tried any," I mutter.

"Surely she has something with chocolate."

Like me, my father is a bit of a chocoholic.

"She has so many great flavors," Michelle says to my dad. "There's chocolate-raspberry, matcha cheesecake, passionfruit, Vietnamese coffee, strawberry-lychee, green tea, Hong Kong milk tea..."

"So it's an Asian ice cream shop?" Mom says.

"Yes," I say.

"Hmm."

"What are we waiting for?" Dad asks. "Let's go. I can't wait to meet this woman."

"I can't wait for you to meet her, either," I say sarcastically.

"Don't worry," Mom says. "We won't scare her off."

Yeah, right. "Why don't we just stay here and talk about your trip?"

"You know what Hong Kong is like. You've been there before. But I've never met your new girlfriend."

As my family parades out the door, I send a quick text to Chloe, warning her that this meet-the-parents business is happening much, much sooner than expected.

Outside, Michelle skips ahead with my parents, and I hang back with Adrienne.

"I can't believe you told Mom and Dad," I say. "You knew this would happen."

My sister shrugs innocently. "I can't believe you bribed my daughter with ice cream. Two ice creams in one day! What were you thinking? You deserve this."

"But Chloe doesn't," I say.

"I really want to meet her."

"We've been on one date. One! And there probably won't be a second date, after she meets all of you."

"If she really likes you, this shouldn't matter."

Does Chloe really like me? What do I want with her?

I don't know exactly, but I'd been hoping to figure it out without any family interference.

Alas…

I'M HANDING a bubble waffle with taro and ginger ice cream to a teenage couple when Drew walks into Ginger Scoops.

I can't help smiling. I just saw him a few hours ago, but I'm so happy to see him again, and when I remember how he kissed his way down my body this morning, I can't help a sharp intake of breath.

Drew is closely followed by an older East Asian couple and a woman in her thirties who's holding Michelle's hand. The older man bears a striking resemblance to Drew.

Wait a second. These must be his parents and sister.

He brought his family to see me? After one date?

What kind of man does that?

The sort of man who gets vilified in a book about ice cream sandwiches, apparently. I'd thought Lisa Mathieson's comments about "Marvin Wong" being completely out of touch with other people's feelings were an exaggeration, but a guy who brings his family to meet a woman after a first date seems pretty out of touch. I haven't had a proper relationship in ages, and I'm not even sure what I want right now…and he's springing a meet-the-parents situation on me?

Ugh.

I frown as he approaches the counter. I should try to be upbeat for his family, but I can't manage it.

"I'm sorry," he says. "My parents insisted on coming to meet you after Michelle told them about our date, and I couldn't talk them out of it. Did you get my text?"

"No, I've been too busy to check my phone."

He looks uncomfortable and apologetic.

Okay. I believe him.

After all, this doesn't seem like the sort of thing Drew would do.

"Aren't you going to introduce us?" his mom asks.

He sighs. "Mom and Dad, this is Chloe. Chloe, these are my parents, Lawrence and Carol, and my sister, Adrienne."

"Uh. Hi. Nice to meet you," I stammer.

"She looks young," Carol says to Drew, then turns back to me. "How old are you?"

"Twenty-five?"

I don't know why it comes out as a question. But I'm rather intimidated by his mother. She looks me over with assessing eyes, as though trying to decide whether I'm good enough for her precious son.

"See, Po Po?" Michelle says. "I told you she was really pretty."

"Yes." Carols sniffs. "And good hips for having children."

My eyes bug out of my head.

This is too much, too soon.

"Actually, it's the shape of the pelvis that matters," Adrienne says, "and can you please not scare her?"

"I'm not scared?" I say, but it doesn't sound convincing. At all.

"I will have a black coffee, as usual," Drew says, as though trying to get the conversation back on track.

"Oh, come on," Lawrence slaps him on the back. "Live a little. Try some ice cream." He looks at me with a kind twinkle in his eye.

He must have been quite the charmer back in the day. He and Drew definitely look alike, but unlike Drew, Lawrence seems like the sort who smiles easily.

"Just the coffee," Drew says.

"I'll have a bubble waffle with ginger and passionfruit!" Michelle says.

"No, you will not," Adrienne says. "Did you think you'd get that one past me? Those waffles are huge. You can get the kiddie size. I hope that's what Drew has been getting you when he brings you here."

"It is," he says.

"Really, I shouldn't let you have any ice cream," Adrienne says to her daughter, "since you had it twice yesterday. But I don't see how I can say no now that we're here. No other treats during the week, okay?"

"Does chocolate count as a treat?" Michelle asks.

"Chocolate most certainly does count as a treat."

"What about dark chocolate? Not much sugar!"

"We'll discuss this later." Adrienne turns to me. "I will have a cone with passionfruit ice cream and strawberry-lychee sorbet."

"Can I have mine in a cone, Mommy?"

"Sure, but it has to be a kiddie-sized serving."

"I will have a cone with passionfruit and ginger," Michelle says. "Make it as big as possible, please."

"Michelle!"

"It was a joke. Chloe knew it was a joke, didn't you, Chloe?"

I can't manage to get any words out. Seeing Drew with his family is terrifying, but it also fills me with a sense of longing, especially when I see Michelle with her mother.

Once upon a time, I had that, too.

Now, I feel like I'm on the outside looking in, and I will always be on the outside.

There's an odd pressure in my chest, and I glance at the photo on the wall, even though I'm too far away to see it clearly.

"I will have a waffle with Vietnamese coffee and chocolate-raspberry," Lawrence says.

"Can I try some of yours?" Michelle asks.

"Of course, sweetie."

"Don't let her try any of the coffee ice cream," Adrienne says. "Knowing my daughter, she'll love the taste of coffee, and she'll be addicted to it before her seventh birthday."

"I just want some of Gung Gung's chocolate-raspberry," Michelle says. "I tried the coffee ice cream last weekend. It was yucky."

"Thank God," Adrienne mutters.

"I'm going to start making the waffle, since it takes a few minutes." I head to the waffle iron and pour in the batter and try to compose myself. When I return to the counter, I ask Carol for her order.

"Surprise me," she says.

Oh, no. I feel like this is some kind of test as to whether I'm good enough for Drew. I look at him, hoping for some help, although what he could provide, I don't know. He gives me a closed-lip smile.

"Um, okay," I say. "Would you like it in a cone or cup or bubble waffle?"

"Cone, I guess."

I'm scooping out Michelle's ice cream when Valerie emerges from the back room.

"Can I help anyone who hasn't ordered yet?" she asks. "Oh, hi, Drew."

"Hello," he says.

"How was last night? And this morning? Chloe hasn't told me much yet. Must have been a good night if you're here again so soon."

My cheeks flame. "Valerie," I hiss.

"You spent the night together after your first date?" Carol turns to her son. "That's no way to treat a nice girl."

So I'm a nice girl? Or does his mother secretly think I'm a slut?

"Have you forgotten our first date?" Lawrence pulls Carol toward him.

"Lawrence!" But she can't help smiling at the memory.

God, I miss seeing my parents tease each other. Not about things like this, not in front of me, but it was always easy to believe my parents were in love.

Now, I'm used to seeing my father all alone.

"Are these your parents, Drew?" Valerie asks.

"Unfortunately, yes."

"Oops."

I hand Michelle her cone, then grab another cone for Drew's mother. I decide on the ginger plus strawberry-lychee sorbet.

Ginger ice cream was my mother's absolute favorite, hence the name of the shop.

Valerie takes out the bubble waffle and folds it into a cone shape, and I scoop ice cream into it. Chocolate-raspberry and Vietnamese coffee. I hope I got that right. My hands are shaking as I hand it over to Lawrence.

"We're really not that frightening," he says.

I attempt a smile, but inside, I'm full of complicated feelings. Perhaps I'm not ready for dating after all.

I ring up their order, then wonder if they'll expect to get their ice cream for free.

"I'll pay for it." Drew slaps some bills on the counter.

"No, I've got it." Lawrence shoves some cash at me before I can say anything. "Lovely to meet you, Chloe. Please join us if you have a spare moment so we can interrogate you."

Drew gives him a dark look. "There will not be any interrogating."

"Clearly we didn't do a good enough job with the last one," Carol says. "Apparently I need to ask any prospective brides—"

"Mom—"

"—whether they intend to write a book about my son." She turns to me. "Do you have any intention of writing a book about Drew?"

"No."

"What about a song, or a movie, or—"

"Maybe I'll name an ice cream flavor after him," I say.

Everyone—except Drew—bursts into laughter, and I feel a little better.

Michelle's eyes light up. "I have so many ideas for ice cream flavors. Could I tell you about them?"

"Another time," Adrienne says. "We need to sit down so you can eat your ice cream before it melts." She leads everyone to a table far from the counter.

Drew stays back, and as he leans closer to me, the air seems to change, and I catch a hint of his scent. Just a few hours ago, we were pressed skin-against-skin in twisted sheets.

"I'm sorry," he says. "They arrived at my condo unannounced, wanting to meet you. Hopefully their curiosity has been satisfied and this will not happen again."

Does that mean he never wants me to see his parents again, because he doesn't want anything serious?

I'm so confused about what's happening, and so confused about what I want. And caught off-guard by the feelings his family inspired in me.

"Are you okay, Chloe?" He brushes my cheek with his hand.

"I'm fine." I give him a smile that I hope is reassuring.

"We're still on for tonight?"

"Yes."

"How about I make you something for dinner?"

"Sure. That would be nice, yes." I can't help a genuine smile now. It's been a long time since someone I've dated has cooked dinner for me. "Are you a good cook?"

"You'll just have to wait and see." He winks at me before joining his family.

I take a deep breath, then turn to help the next group in line.

Sarah walks into Ginger Scoops just after six o'clock.

"The strawberry-rhubarb pie wasn't very popular today." She lifts up the pie in her hand. "Anyone want some?"

"Oh my God, thank you. That's just what I need." I grab a plate and serve myself a large piece of pie with a scoop of ginger ice cream, then start shoveling it into my mouth as Valerie and Sarah look on. "I've had A Day."

"She met her new boyfriend's parents," Valerie explains to Sarah.

"Wow, you move fast. I thought Josh and I moved fast, but you have us beat. Will you be engaged by the end of the week? Married by July?"

I almost spit strawberry-rhubarb pie onto the table.

"No, seriously. How was the date?" Sarah asks. "When are you seeing him next? And why on earth have you already met his parents?"

"Yes," Valerie says. "You've been holding out on me. I need details."

My friends sit at the table with me and help themselves to pie.

"We went to that new place off College," I say. "S-slash-E."

"Such a dumb name," Valerie says around a mouthful of pie.

"It was good," I say. "Good food, good drinks."

"And good company?"

"Well, I went home with him. So…you know."

Valerie motions for me to continue. "How does he look without a shirt? How was he in bed? "

I try to suppress my smile, but I can't. "It was really amazing."

"So amazing that he brought his family to meet you today?" Sarah asks.

"They, um, heard he went on a date and showed up at his condo and demanded to meet me? I'm not sure. Wasn't his idea."

Emotion clogs my throat as I remember seeing his niece and her mother together. His niece calling her grandparents "Po Po" and "Gung Gung," like I used to call my maternal grandparents. The way they affectionately bickered.

The way it made me feel incredibly lonely.

Even now, surrounded my friends, I feel a little alone.

I swallow the words I want to say. Though I did say some of them to Drew last weekend. When he's around, especially when he's holding me, that feeling starts to dissipate.

I need to see him. Now.

I polish off my pie and jump up. "I'll clean up, and then I'll be out of here."

"Wow, the sex must really be amazing," Valerie says.

Normally, I would think of a retort, but my mind is already somewhere else.

Specifically, Drew's bed.

I'M PRETTY sure I blew Chloe's mind last night, but after the unicorn nightmare fiasco this morning and the unexpected meet-the-parents incident this afternoon, I consider myself lucky that she's coming over again tonight.

I'm dreadfully out of practice with this dating business.

When the phone rings and she asks me to buzz her up, my heart starts doing some kind of freaky rhythm in my chest—again, I assume this is because I'm out of practice.

When she enters my apartment, I greet her with a searing kiss. I longed to do that all afternoon, but of course I wouldn't have kissed her in front of my family.

"Hey, you" she says. "What are you making for dinner?"

"Lasagna."

"I love lasagna. Did you make it from scratch?"

"I did."

"Impressive."

"Maybe you should wait until you try it to say that."

She rests her hands on my shoulders and grins at me, and I feel so damn lucky. She's wearing a purple shirt and jeans. Nothing fancy, but she's gorgeous all the same. Her hair is tied up in a ponytail, but a few strands have escaped. I brush them behind her ear.

We sit down to eat a few minutes later. I serve her a generous piece of lasagna and some green salad, and when she tries the lasagna, she almost looks like she's having an orgasm.

I can say that because I know exactly how she looks when she orgasms.

I'm a very lucky man.

After dinner, I invite her to raid my chocolate stash.

"You have a chocolate stash?"

"I'm very serious about my chocolate."

We kneel down to look at my dedicated chocolate cupboard. Mostly dark chocolate—that's the good stuff. I have bars of seventy and eight-five percent cocoa, and boxes of fine imported chocolates.

"Oh my God," she says. "You're every girl's dream. You make an amazing cheesy lasagna, and you have a chocolate cupboard."

All of a sudden, my smile feels a bit forced. "I was left at the altar and there's an entire chapter in a bestselling book about how I'm a grumpy bastard."

"I finished the book."

I stiffen. "And yet you're still here."

She shrugs. "Yeah."

Maybe she just wants a bit of fun in the bedroom, and I'm providing that, and she doesn't care about my bad qualities because she doesn't want anything long-term with me.

I don't know how to feel about that.

"I shouldn't have chocolate," she says. "I already had strawberry-rhubarb pie and ginger ice cream today."

"Just a square." I take out a half-finished bar of dark chocolate, break off a piece, and hold it up to her lips. She has a bite and groans appreciatively, sounding, once again, like she's having an orgasm.

I finish the chocolate then haul her into my arms. "That's it. We're going to bed."

"But I wanted to carefully examine the rest of your chocolate stash."

"I want to carefully examine every inch of your body."

"Well, in that case... Just grab my purse on the way to the bedroom, okay?"

I do as requested before carrying her into my bedroom and setting her down on my bed. I like the look of her there.

"What's in your purse?"

"Toys."

Oh.

She pulls out a small vibrator and a dildo and places them on my sheets. Both toys are bright pink.

"These are what you used when you were thinking about me?" I ask.

"Yes. Are you intimidated?"

"Why the fuck would I be intimidated?"

"I don't know. Some men are weird about sex toys."

"I promise I'm not one of them."

No, this is going to be a hell of a lot of fun. My cock is hard, pressing against the zipper of my jeans.

I reach for the bottom of her shirt at exactly the same time as she reaches for mine. We pull off our shirts, and then I slip off her bra and unveil her breasts. I circle my tongue over one nipple as I brush the other with my thumb, and she arches against me.

A toy can't suck her nipples. A toy can't be skin-against-skin with her.

But, yeah, this is going to be fun.

I shove down her pants along with her panties and slip two fingers inside her.

"You're already wet, baby."

She nods helplessly.

I take the dildo and slide it inside her slick channel. She shudders.

"Too much?" I ask.

"No...no."

I hand her the vibrator. "Now make yourself come. Can you do that for me?"

She puts the vibrator to her clit and turns it on, and...oh, fuck. Her other hand goes to her breast and squeezes, and her eyes flutter shut.

"No, Chloe. Watch me."

I push up from the bed and slide off my jeans and boxers. I stroke my cock and enjoy the way her gaze follows my hand, enjoy the way she licks her lips.

The other toy is sticking out of her. I can see her pussy lips wrapped around it.

God, it's hot that she's doing this in front of me.

Her breaths get louder as she continues to use the vibrator, and her gaze stays on me as I stroke myself. Slowly. Any faster, and I would lose my goddamn mind.

Another minute and she squeezes her eyes shut and grips the sheets with her other hand.

"*Drew.*"

I'm not touching her, but she's coming for *me*, and I love it.

She turns off the vibrator and sets it aside. "I need you."

Lazily, I move the dildo in and out of her a few times. "I could leave you here with the toy inside of you and order you to stay put as I did the dishes, surfed the internet, read a book... Would you like that?"

"Sounds like torture."

"Would you do it for me?"

"Yes, but don't you dare do it right now."

I wouldn't.

I roll on a condom and remove the toy. It glistens with her moisture. I put it aside, then push myself inside her.

Oh, God.

She clutches my shoulders and breathes heavily beneath me. We begin to move together, my slick skin against hers. I slip one hand underneath to grab her ass, and with the other, I cup her cheek. She feels so amazing, and she looks so amazing, her dark hair spread out on my pillow.

Like she belongs here.

I thrust in and out of her, again and again, and she holds me close. This time, when her orgasm overtakes her, she clenches around me and shakes beneath me as she cries out my name.

It's so perfect, I can barely stand it.

She rolls us over so she's riding me, and I love looking up at her and touching her breasts. I love seeing our bodies joined.

When she lowers her chest to mine and increases her pace, I finish inside her.

We hold each other afterward, as daylight fades and the room darkens. We're still naked, limbs intertwined.

Chloe slides her hand through my hair. "When your family was at Ginger Scoops—"

"Again, I'm so sorry about that."

"I mean, yeah, it was a bit much, but I liked seeing them. Except I desperately wanted to feel like I belonged, and I didn't. Which makes sense, of course. I've only met them once, and you and I, well…it hasn't been very long." She shakes her head. "Forget about it."

No, I'm not going to forget about anything she says.

I'm suddenly overcome with the desire to give her the family she doesn't have anymore. To make her feel like part of my own.

That desire shakes me to the core.

I swore off serious relationships, yet that seems to be what I want with Chloe.

How did this happen?

Even if I want a relationship, how on earth could I possibly make it work? How could I give her everything she needs?

I think of Lisa's book, with its stupid ice cream sandwich on the cover. I've tried not to let it get to me too much. I've tried to focus on the ridiculous descriptions of ice cream sandwiches with oatmeal-raisin cookies and mocha ice cream, the "mysterious and a little exotic" line about black sesame ice cream. I've tried to think of the book as utterly ridiculous and stupid.

But underneath all that, I fear Lisa was right about me being a terrible partner.

There's one line in particular that haunts me. It haunted me when I first read the Marvin Wong chapter a year ago, and it haunts me even more now, especially after I started things up with Chloe.

I'm not sure I can do this again, and I'm not sure it would be fair to Chloe to try.

She takes a deep breath and turns around so we're spooning.

"This feels so good," she says.

It does.

I don't need to make any decisions yet. It's only been two days. For now, I'll just focus on how wonderful it feels to be with her.

On Monday, Chloe's day off, she comes to see me after dinner, and we have sex and watch a romantic comedy on Netflix. The movie is stupid and contrived, but it still makes me laugh.

If I'm being honest with myself, it also stirs some goddamn *feelings* in my chest.

I am mildly annoyed by this.

Tuesday, we don't have plans to see each other. I think this is smart. After spending three nights in a row together, it's time to have some space.

When I get home from work, I pick up the gruesome thriller that I started a while back, but it doesn't hold my interest. Instead, all I can think about is Chloe, and then, for some strange reason, Havarti Sparkles pops into my mind.

My brain is so weird.

You know what? I can visit Chloe at Ginger Scoops. Just to have coffee and talk with her for a few minutes. Nothing big. It's only a ten-minute walk.

My heart beats with anticipation as I near Baldwin Street. When I open the door, the chimes tinkle, and Chloe smiles at me from behind the counter.

"Drew!" she says as I approach. "I didn't expect to see you today."

"Just thought I'd pop in for a coffee."

"Are you absolutely sure I can't interest you in some ice cream?"

You know what?

"Sure, why not?" I say, as though it's no big deal.

She grins. "Really?"

"I definitely want a coffee, but I'll try a sample of ice cream, too."

She scoops a tiny amount of Vietnamese coffee ice cream onto a green plastic spoon. "Here you go."

There's a spark when our fingers touch.

I lift the spoon to my face and peer at it suspiciously. Once, I associated ice cream with happy childhood memories, and then I associated it with the failure of my engagement and a bestselling book that portrayed me as an asshole.

Now, I'm starting to associate it with Chloe.

I slide the spoon into my mouth and brace myself.

The moment is anti-climactic.

The ice cream isn't bad. I don't gag or spit it out. It's sweet and rather refreshing, though I can't fully appreciate it.

"What's the verdict?" Chloe asks. "You can tell me you hate it. It's okay."

"I didn't hate it," I say, and that kind of feels like a big deal. "But I didn't love it, either. I don't need a whole cup."

"Not even kiddie size?"

"Not even kiddie size." I hate to disappoint her, but I'm not going to lie.

"Would you like to try another flavor? Maybe chocolate-raspberry? Or perhaps you'd prefer a sorbet." She leans across the counter and squeezes my hand.

I'm considering my options when Chloe's face suddenly lights up. She's not looking at me, though. She's looking at something over my shoulder.

"Aunt Anita!" she exclaims, then rushes around the counter.

I turn and see an Asian woman, maybe Chinese, in her late forties or early fifties, accompanied by a slightly younger black woman. Chloe reaches her aunt and throws her arms around her. She's mentioned an aunt before, her mother's sister who lives in New York.

I smile because it makes me happy to see Chloe happy, but I feel like she doesn't need me and my family anymore, now that her aunt is here.

I shake my head and tell myself to stop being so fucking insecure.

When Chloe steps back, she places her hand on my lower back. "This is Drew. We're...seeing each other."

I feel a mixture of relief and disappointment that she doesn't call me her boyfriend.

"Drew, this is my aunt, Anita, and...?" She looks at Anita questioningly, tilting her head toward the other woman.

"My wife, Deidre."

By the look on her face, the existence of Anita's wife is a shock to Chloe.

I think this family stuff will be easier for Chloe to handle by herself, rather than with a guy she's only been seeing for a few days.

"It's nice to meet you," I say, shaking hands with the two women before I turn to Chloe. "But I should be going. I just stopped in to say hello. Text me later, okay?"

She kisses me on the cheek.

I return home, where I read about dead bodies and disturbing serial killers. Usually this would be my kind of thing, but I can't help wishing I were at Ginger Scoops instead.

I CAN'T BELIEVE Aunt Anita got married without telling me.

Married!

I didn't know she was engaged. I didn't even know she was seeing someone seriously.

It's not a shock that she's with a woman, though. When I was five, my aunt brought a woman to Toronto to meet her family. Before they came, my mom explained to me that although a couple was often a man and a woman, it didn't have to be. Two men or two women could be together, and that was totally fine.

I was a bit confused, but mainly just annoyed that my mother had interrupted me. I was very busy drawing a picture of Santa's workshop. I hoped Aunt Anita would bring me good presents. She traveled all over the world for work, and usually she brought me nice things.

I have only a vague memory of the woman she brought home with her that Christmas, and then again that summer. We never saw her after that. I do remember that my aunt brought me an awesome Lego set.

When I was twelve, Mom told me that Aunt Anita was

coming to Toronto for Chinese New Year and bringing a man with her.

I furrowed my brow in confusion. "I thought she was a lesbian."

"Occasionally she dates men, too," Mom said.

"You can do that?"

Mom nodded. "She's bi. She likes both."

That totally blew my mind. I hadn't realized there was a word for it. I thought you had to choose.

I'd known I wasn't gay. I liked boys, so that must mean I was straight, right?

But sometimes, I liked girls, too. I had a bit of a crush on my friend Kara, and I was obsessed with Catherine Zeta-Jones. I thought she was so hot in *Chicago*, which I watched over and over. Sometimes, I even imagined kissing her.

I'd been confused, but suddenly, it all made sense.

"Mom," I said, "I think that's what I am, too."

She hesitated, just for a moment. "Okay. Why do you think that?"

So I told her, a little embarrassed because this didn't seem like the sort of thing you usually told your mom. But she was pretty awesome about it. She didn't say it was just a phase and I'd change my mind when I was older, or anything like that.

I didn't so much come out to my mother as realize I was bi while talking to her.

And I suspect she wouldn't have been quite so good about it if it hadn't been for Aunt Anita.

My dad, on the other hand, wasn't entirely comfortable with my proclamation, but I only knew that because I heard him talking to my mother later that night.

Now, thirteen years later, my aunt has brought someone else to meet her family.

A wife.

"When did you get married?" I ask.

"Last week," Anita says. "We're on our honeymoon. Toronto, then Montreal and Quebec City. Deidre's never been before."

She takes her wife's hand and squeezes it.

My aunt is all smiles, and I'm glad she's happy.

But I'm also furious.

Aunt Anita is the only family I have on my mother's side, and although she hasn't lived in Toronto since I was a baby, she used to visit several times a year and we were always close. When I was a teenager, sometimes it was easier to talk to her than my parents. She got me in ways that my parents didn't, better understood certain things I was dealing with.

Since my mother's funeral, though, she's only been to Toronto once, and that was when my grandmother died.

We don't talk much, either. Many of the emails I send her go unanswered. She did loan me some money for Ginger Scoops and helped me a little with my business plan, but when I sent her pictures of it the day it opened, she didn't respond.

After I lost my mom, I desperately wished for Anita to be part of my life, and she wasn't.

I don't say this now, though.

"Does my dad know you're here?" I ask.

She nods. "We're all having dinner on Thursday."

"I have to work."

"Valerie said it would be okay if you couldn't be here tonight and Thursday night."

"You talked to my employee?"

Valerie pops out from behind the counter. "She emailed me a few days ago." She smiles. "Now, what would everyone like to eat? You can't come here and not try the ice cream. I mean, unless you're Drew."

"I got him to try the Vietnamese coffee this afternoon," I say.

"How did he enjoy it?"

"Um. Well. He tolerated it, I guess."

And then he left soon after my aunt arrived, as though

understanding it would be easier this way for me. Drew and I are still getting to know one another, and navigating this situation with him here would be more than my poor brain could handle.

Maybe, once we've been together a while, I would find strength from his presence at a time like this, but…

I can't believe I'm thinking about being with him long-term. Where did that come from?

"Vietnamese coffee ice cream sounds good," Anita says, startling me out of my thoughts. "What else should I try?"

"Matcha cheesecake," I suggest.

"I'll have the taro and strawberry-lychee," Deidre says.

"Bubble waffles?" Valerie asks.

"Sure," Anita says. "Why not."

"I'll bring you something, too," Valerie says, her hand on my shoulder.

I take a seat at a table by the window, Anita and Deidre across from me. Deidre looks around, a smile on her face, and I feel a bit self-conscious. It's my ice cream parlor, after all.

"Keisha would love this place," she says, patting the head of the rocking unicorn.

"She would," Anita agrees.

"Who's Keisha?" I ask.

My aunt pulls out her phone and shows me a picture of herself with Deidre and three children, who must be Deidre's. Twin girls and a boy.

"Keisha, Sasha, and Isaac," Deidre says, pointing at them with a fond smile. "The twins are six, and Isaac is eight."

Their skin is lighter in color than their mother's—I think their father is white. Biracial, then, like me. Except growing up with a black mother and white father in the US is probably quite different from having an Asian mother and a white father in Canada.

"They're cute," I say.

"They're with their father this week, but they live with me most of the time."

I'm trying to imagine my aunt as a stepmother. They'd be my step-cousins—is that a thing? It's hard to wrap my mind around all of this.

"Hopefully we'll bring them to Toronto in a few months," Anita says.

So now she wants to see me regularly, after three years of not visiting?

Valerie comes over with our ice cream. She's gotten me a scoop of chocolate-raspberry and a scoop of ginger in a cup. Anita hands her twenty bucks. "Keep the change."

"You don't—"

"I insist." Anita presses the money into Valerie's palm, then starts on her ice cream. After complimenting my skills as an ice cream artisan, she dips her spoon into Deidre's bubble waffle and tries the strawberry-lychee sorbet.

They're both smiling lots, looking like the honeymooning couple that they are. I decide not to share my other feelings with my aunt. I certainly can't do it when Deidre is present.

But Anita says to me, "We'll have dinner tonight. Just the two of us, like old times."

Whenever she visited, we'd always spend one whole day together. We'd do fun things like take the ferry to Centre Island or go to Canada's Wonderland, the amusement park north of the city. In the evening, we'd go out to eat, something I rarely did with my parents. Anita was my cool aunt, and I loved it when she came to town.

"You're on your honeymoon," I protest. "You can't ditch your wife."

"I'll be fine," Deidre says. "I'll hang out with some of Anita's old friends, and she'll join me later."

Well, then. Apparently they have this all planned out.

"I take it you're surprised," Anita says.

"Of course I'm surprised," I say.

We're at Boreal, a restaurant that calls itself a "Canadian bistro." I ordered the venison, and my aunt ordered us a charcuterie board to start. It's sitting on the table, but I haven't touched it yet.

The restaurant isn't busy, and we have a quiet corner at the back. Anita knows the owner. How, I'm not sure. She hasn't lived in Toronto for over two decades, but she always seems to know lots of people—I remember that about her. When I was younger, we'd often end up at restaurants where she knew the owner.

It's like old times, and yet it isn't.

"How long have you and Deidre been together?" I ask.

"Less than a year," she says.

"And you're already married?" That seems fast to me.

She shrugs. "When you're my age, when you've been around for a while...you know what you want, and you don't waste time."

"How do you get along with her kids?"

"Keisha and I have gotten along well from the beginning. It's been a little tougher with Sasha and Isaac, but it's getting better."

"Have you lived with them yet? Or not until you get home from your honeymoon?"

"We've lived together for four months. Since we got engaged." She smiles. "I always wanted to have children but never got around to it. Now, I have everything."

"You didn't tell me. You didn't invite me to your wedding."

"It wasn't a proper wedding. It..." She sighs, then picks up a slice of bread and tops it with some kind of cured meat—the server told us what everything was, but I don't remember. It wasn't important enough to register in my brain.

"You're all I have left of my mother's family. You used to visit all the time, but you weren't there..." *You weren't there when I needed you.* "I'm angry."

I don't usually tell people when I'm angry at them; I hide my feelings behind a cheerful front. But I can't help it, not now.

"Why?" I ask, then cram my mouth with cured meat.

"I stayed away for so long. It would have been weird to just show up all of a sudden."

"Like you did today."

"Like I did today." She pauses. "I lost both my parents and my sister in the span of three years."

"I know." I lost them, too. My mother and my grandparents, all so close together. "But didn't you want to see the family you had left?"

"It became too hard to go to Toronto, and when you emailed me and suggested you could come to New York, I was in a really bad place. I was trying to keep my life from breaking at the seams. I was afraid that if I saw you, I would completely lose it and wouldn't be able to get out of bed for a month."

"Why would that have happened?"

Anita shakes her head. "You look so much like your mother. Your mannerisms are the same, too. I wanted to see you but knew it would remind me too much of what I'd lost." She has a sip of her wine. "My response has always been to run away. I left Toronto twenty-four years ago because my best friend passed away and I couldn't stand to be here anymore."

God. I let that sink in. "I'm sorry."

"*I'm* sorry, Chloe. I'm so sorry. I wish I hadn't been such a basket case after Sandra died. I wish I'd been stronger."

"But you're better now. With Deidre."

She nods, then reaches across the table and squeezes my hand before helping herself to some of the cured meat. "I won't disappear on you again."

"Okay," I whisper.

"I'll come back in August or September, I promise. With or

without Deidre's family—my family. I'm not sure yet if they'll be able to come. You can visit me in New York anytime. Maybe in the fall or winter, when it's not ice cream season?"

"Yes. That would be nice. I haven't been to New York since I was a teenager." Mom took me to visit my aunt and eat our way through the city. It was an exhausting trip. Mom and I argued every day about the stupidest things.

I miss her so much.

I miss the relationship we would have had when I was an adult.

So much shit has happened, but somehow, I will find a way through.

Thursday, I leave Ginger Scoops early so I can have dinner with Dad, Anita, and Deidre. Dad has us all over and grills steaks and vegetables. When we're digging into the spiced apple pie and ginger ice cream I brought for dessert, Anita says, "You didn't bring Drew tonight. Has he met your father yet?"

I shake my head.

"Who's Drew?" Dad asks.

"Sorry," Anita says. "I assumed you knew."

"The guy I'm seeing," I explain. "He was at Ginger Scoops when Anita and Deidre showed up." I shoot my aunt a glare that turns into a smile. I can't say I'm mad at her for spilling the beans. I don't usually share details of my dating life with my father, but it's not a big deal.

"What does he do?" Dad asks.

"He works in finance."

"Ah. Good."

"His dad's parents are from Toisan, but his dad was born here." I turn to Anita again. "Like you and Mom."

We're all silent for a moment after the mention of my mother.

Dad clears his throat. "How did you meet him?"

"He comes to Ginger Scoops with his niece."

I imagine my aunt bringing me to an ice cream shop like Ginger Scoops when I was a child—it's the sort of thing she would have done when she was in town. Except back then, I don't remember there being any Asian ice cream shops.

"Does he look after his niece a lot?" Dad asks.

"For a while, he was looking after her every Saturday."

"Sounds like he'd make a good father."

I choke on my apple pie.

Dad laughs. I think he was hoping for that kind of reaction. "But to be clear, you don't owe me grandchildren."

"I want kids," I say. "Just don't expect them anytime soon."

He smiles at me, and I look away.

He says I don't owe him grandchildren, like that isn't his business, and yet he still keeps insisting that I study dentistry.

When I told Aunt Anita about my feelings, it went well. I want to be honest with my father, too. I want to tell him that there's no way I'm becoming a dentist and I don't want him to keep bringing it up. I want to tell him that his comment about how he didn't see Mom as Chinese bothered me. I doubt he remembers making that comment, but it's stuck in my brain.

I want to tell him that I love him, but it still feels like he doesn't really see me.

So when Anita and Deidre head to their hotel, I stay behind with my father. I help him wash dishes, and then we sit at the kitchen table with cups of tea.

"Chloe…" He reaches for my hand, but he doesn't look at me.

He's crying.

"Dad." I squeeze his hand.

"I shouldn't cry," he says. "It's been years, but sometimes, it feels like yesterday."

Grief isn't linear; it isn't constantly decreasing in strength.

Most of the time now, it's bearable for me, but there are still moments when it's overwhelming.

"I'm glad Anita came," Dad says. "I'm happy for her. But…" His shoulders shake.

Tonight is not the time to have the conversation I wanted to have.

That's okay. It can wait.

We sit at the table together for a long, long time.

After I leave my father's, I don't feel like going home and being alone, so I head to Drew's. He buzzes me up.

When he greets me at the door, I take his hand and head to the bedroom, where I kick off my pants and climb into bed. He does the same and wraps his arms around me.

I feel safe.

I tell him about the past few days, about Anita and my father, about the years since my mother's car was hit by a tractor trailer.

I tell him about how my dad said Drew would make a good father and that made me choke on my pie. I feel Drew stiffen slightly behind me, but he doesn't say anything.

Perhaps I shouldn't have brought that up. We've been together such a short time.

Still, I feel close to him in a way I haven't felt with anyone for quite a while. I thought I wouldn't be able to do this again. I thought that part of me was broken.

I was wrong.

Who would have thought an ice cream-hating finance guy would make me feel like this?

I look at Havarti Sparkles, sitting on his bedside table, and smile.

"What can I do for you?" Drew asks.

"Just stay here with me."

"I can do that."

"If you've got a unicorn onesie, you could put that on, too. It would make me laugh."

"Unicorn onesies? They make those for adults?" The expression of horror on his face is priceless.

"They do!"

"Let me guess. You own one?"

"No, but maybe I'll buy you one as a gift."

"Speaking of gifts…" He climbs out of bed and grabs a small package wrapped in blue paper from his dresser. "I was going to give this to you on the weekend, but you can have it now."

He got me a present! My chest feels painfully tight. I tear open the paper to reveal an amigurumi eggplant…and an amigurumi peach.

I burst into laughter.

And then I hug him and kiss him like I never want to let him go.

Where are we going? I'm not sure, but maybe it's all going to be okay.

[18]

DREW

I DON'T KNOW what I'm doing.

Really, I have no idea.

Wednesday after work, I went to the Hall of Horrors—otherwise known as Libby's Gifts—to buy amigurumi for Chloe. Fortunately, I didn't have any nightmares about unicorns or Hello Kitty afterward.

I thought I'd only do something like that for Michelle, but nope, I went there for Chloe, too. When she opened my gift and laughed, I couldn't contain my joy, and when she shed a few tears as she talked about her mom and her family, there were some painful stirrings in a body part that I think is called a heart.

Which surprised me, because I've been accused of not having a heart.

And when she told me how her dad had joked that I'd make a good father, I managed to suppress my urge to run out the door.

That one hit too close to home.

But I zipped my mouth shut and stuffed any retorts deep inside me. I couldn't stop my body from going rigid, though, and I knew she felt it, but she didn't say anything.

Chloe is an affectionate person, and I love how she always

wants to touch me, even when we're in public. She seems so...pure.

Not innocent, no, and it's not like she's been untouched by suffering, but there's something about her laughter and delight in the world around her that seems pure to me. I can't help wanting to spend as much time as I can with Chloe.

Even though I seriously doubt I'm any good for her.

Still, I ask her to stay the night on Thursday, and I ask her to come over again on Saturday after she's finished work, so I can lose myself in her body.

Sunday, I meet Chloe at Ginger Scoops at seven, planning to take her to a cider bar on Ossington with a nice backyard patio.

My jaw drops when I see her. She's not wearing jeans and a simple T-shirt, like she usually wears when she's working. No, she's changed into a cute sundress, printed with yellow flowers, that skims her knees.

"Ready?" I ask, my voice rough.

"Yep, let's go drink some cider!"

Frankly, I'd prefer my bedroom. I want to slip those straps off her shoulders and suck on her nipples and do all the activities that people think of when they see eggplant and peach emojis. Or amigurumi.

After she locks the door to Ginger Scoops, I capture her mouth in mine and kiss her deeply. "You look hot."

She steps back and looks me up and down appreciatively. "You're not so bad yourself."

When we reach Spadina, I realize I'm holding her hand. How did that happen? I don't remember consciously doing it. But it feels right, and I don't let go.

It's a little ways to Ossington, but it's a beautiful night and we decide to walk, holding hands the whole time.

At the cider bar, I ask to be seated on the patio. We get a small table in the corner and each order a flight of four ciders. Our drinks come quickly, but when I lift my first tasting glass to clink it against hers, she's distracted. She's looking at a couple of women who just walked onto the patio.

"I slept with her," Chloe says with a giggle. "The one on the left."

The woman in question is white, with short pink hair and a nose ring. She has a tattoo snaking up her arm.

"Oh," I say. "When was this?"

"A couple years."

Not super recent. Okay.

Admittedly, this is the first time I've run into a *woman* that my date has slept with.

Chloe puts her hand on my cheek and turns it toward her. "Are you jealous? We slept together a couple times, that's all. It meant nothing."

It meant nothing. Is she implying that it means something with *me*? That I'm different? I hope so, even if I'm not sure she should be feeling this way about me.

I'm not jealous. It was a while ago, and it was nothing serious. It would be utterly ridiculous—and hypocritical—for me to expect the woman I'm seeing to have no past. I like that she has one.

But I can't stand the thought of her seeing anyone else *now*. Although I'm pretty sure she isn't, I want to be clear on the matter.

"I want to be exclusive," I blurt out. "I want you to be mine. Only mine."

She puts her hand on my knee. "I'd like that, too."

I can hardly believe this is happening. I'm having drinks with a beautiful woman, and she wants to be with me.

Me, the villain of *Embrace Your Inner Ice Cream Sandwich*.

"Is this just because I'm amazing in bed?"

"Oh, for God's sake," she says. "Stop being so insecure and cocky at the same time. I don't know how you manage that combination."

I pick up one of my small glasses of cider and lift it in her direction with a smirk.

This is all a bit too good to be true, but for now, I'll just enjoy it.

I have a sip of the first cider. It's tart and refreshing and—

"Drew?" It's a woman's voice. Although it's vaguely familiar, I can't place it. "Or should I say Marvin?"

I turn around and see Lisa's best friend, Rhiannon. Her lips are thin and twisted unkindly. The last time I saw this woman, it was at the wedding that never happened, and she was wearing a bridesmaid dress.

Yeah, it looks like this evening was too good to be true after all.

As I'm sitting there slack-jawed, Chloe holds out her hand. "Hi, I'm Chloe. Drew's girlfriend. Nice to meet you."

Girlfriend.

Rhiannon doesn't bother shaking her hand. "I can't believe you have a girlfriend," she says to me instead.

I can't quite believe it either, but I don't let on that I feel this way.

"Ohhh," Rhiannon says. "She doesn't know, does she?"

I never liked Rhiannon. She was one of those mean girl types, and I'm not sure what Lisa saw in her.

"Know that he's the inspiration for Marvin Wong?" Chloe says. "Yes, I'm aware of that. I read the book."

Rhiannon seems taken aback. "Right."

Her companion—a man who was her boyfriend three years ago and could be her husband now—says nothing but rests his hand on her waist.

"Alright, we better be going," Rhiannon says. "You kids have fun. But, Chloe, I suggest you don't make the same mistake as my best friend."

As soon as she walks away, I chug one of my little glasses of cider.

"Hey." Chloe rests her hand on my knee. "Don't let it ruin our night. I honestly don't care what your ex and her friends think of you."

"Maybe you should," I say, picking up the next glass of cider. "I don't understand why it doesn't bother you. There are tons of men or women you could date who weren't left at the altar and didn't turn out to be the villain in a bestselling memoir."

"It's just bad luck that it happened to you."

"It's not simply bad luck."

"I called you the *inspiration* for Marvin because I suspect it wasn't entirely accurate. Lisa said you were grouchy, and okay, I can see her point, though you're really not that bad. But you're not a bastard who's crushing my spirit and melting my inner ice cream sandwich." She shakes her head. "God, I can't believe I just said that. I'm serious, though. I like being with you, Drew, and I don't feel like you're stopping me from reaching my full potential, like Lisa seems to believe. Maybe you were different with her —it was several years ago. Maybe you weren't well suited. Maybe she exaggerated to make a better story."

I look down. "She did overstate things a bit, but…" I take a deep breath, and I tell Chloe my deepest fear. "Even if the details aren't all correct, I can't help wondering, 'What if she's right?' I think she might be right about me as a person. I bring others down. I'm not a great boyfriend."

I don't mention the thing that haunts me the most, but still, I'm surprised I admitted as much as I did.

"She isn't," Chloe says.

How can she speak with such conviction? She hasn't known me all that long.

"For example," she continues, "you might not like ice cream, you might not exactly understand my desire to run an ice cream shop, but you've never discouraged me. On Thursday night, after I had dinner with my family, you were supportive, as I knew you would be. Beneath that slightly surly exterior, you're kind and thoughtful. I haven't had…" She swallows. "I haven't had a relationship like this in a long time. It's not like I can open up to everyone."

I release the breath I was holding.

"Do you believe me?" she asks, concern in her beautiful face.

I nod.

I do believe her, kind of. I feel better now, though I'm not fully convinced.

But I won't bombard her with my insecurities any further.

Just my luck that in a large city, we somehow ran into a former bed partner of Chloe's and my ex-fiancée's best friend in the same night.

We stay on the patio until ten o'clock, and then we walk back to my place. Now that the sun has gone down, it's cooling off, and I rub Chloe's arms to warm them up. She laughs.

"I'm fine," she says. "Don't worry about me."

And then she kisses me in the middle of the sidewalk.

At home, I push down the straps of her dress, as I've been longing to do all evening, and take her nipples into my mouth. My hand slides up her leg, and I pleasure her until she's trembling in my arms.

Then I do it again. And again.

And then I push inside her.

Afterward, Chloe falls asleep quickly, but I stay awake. For three years, I almost never shared a bed with someone, so this past week has been quite a change. I've generally been sleeping well, but tonight is different. Tonight, my fears from earlier return.

What if I'm bad for her? I couldn't bear it if I drove the spark from her eyes, the spring from her step, and I fear that's what a man like me would inevitably do.

Then there's the issue of children. I know it's too early to be thinking about that, but I can't help it. I suspect Chloe wants children. And I…

Well.

Marvin Wong would make a horrible father.

That's what Lisa wrote in her book.

I finally fall asleep, only to have another vaguely disturbing dream about unicorns.

Tuesday afternoon, I make a new batch of Hong Kong milk tea ice cream. When I come out to the front, a familiar figure is walking toward the counter.

I smile. "Grandma!"

Lillian is behind her, looking a little bigger than the last time I saw her. "Hey, Chloe. It's super cute in here."

Grandma nods, then turns to Lillian. "Your little girl will love it."

I hope I'm still in business when Lillian's child is old enough to toddle across the floor and sit on the rocking unicorn. "You're having a girl?"

"Yes!" Lillian says. "She's giving me enormous cravings for ice cream."

"You came to the right place. You can try samples of anything you like." I gesture to the blackboard that lists the flavors.

"What's taro?" Grandma asks.

"A root vegetable." I point to the tubs. "It's the purple one."

"Purple! That doesn't seem natural."

"Would you like to try it?"

Grandma shakes her head, but Lillian says, "I'll have a taste."

I hand her a spoon with the "unnatural" purple ice cream.

"Hmm. It's pretty good. You should try it, Grandma."

"I'll try the green tea instead."

I hand a sample of green tea ice cream to my grandmother, bracing myself for her response to something that isn't chocolate or butterscotch or vanilla.

To my surprise, her face lights up. "You wouldn't think tea and ice cream would go well together, but they do. This is delicious."

"Thank you."

"I want to try something else. Maybe ginger? I'm skeptical, but if the green tea was good…"

Grandma tries the ginger, strawberry-lychee, Hong Kong milk tea, and Vietnamese coffee. I'd normally limit customers to two samples, but she's my grandmother and we're not busy. Plus, I like how she enjoys every single one, much to my surprise.

This isn't just my grandmother being nice. She's always honest when it comes to food.

"Durian," she says. "That's the spiky fruit, isn't it?"

Everything has gone well so far, but I seriously doubt my grandmother, who makes deviled eggs, meatloaf, and lime Jell-O salad, will enjoy durian.

"It smells really, really bad," I tell her. "Like natural gas."

"But it tastes good?"

"Some people think so. It's Valerie's favorite thing in the world."

"I must try it," she says.

I hand her a sample.

"Oh, God. That smells vile." Lillian turns away, and I'm afraid my pregnant cousin is going to be sick, but she recovers quickly.

Grandma sniffs and makes a face. "I can't believe it's a fruit." She slides the spoon into her mouth, and her eyebrows pop up.

She must be disgusted by this weird Asian stuff. It was bound to happen eventually.

"Wow," she says. "That's amazing."

I stare at her incredulously. "Really?"

"It's your ice cream, Chloe. You must know it's good."

I can't manage a response. My grandmother likes durian ice cream?

"Can I get three flavors in a medium cup?" she asks.

"Sure."

"I'll have the green tea, ginger, and durian."

"I'm not sure I'll be able to sit next to you," Lillian says.

"You'll manage."

I suppress a laugh.

"I'll have the taro, strawberry-lychee, and Hong Kong milk tea," my cousin says as she hands me a twenty.

Valerie takes over at the counter while I sit with my family.

"Your father tells me you have a new man," Grandma says in between bites of green tea ice cream.

"I do. His name is Drew." Although I'm a little annoyed that everyone seems to know about this, I can't help but smile when I say his name.

"This is the first I've heard of it," Lillian says. "You told me at Grandma's party that you were too busy with the store to date."

I shrug. "Sometimes things just happen."

Like my grandmother discovering she enjoys durian ice cream.

She even buys a pint to take home.

That evening, I spend some time in the tiny office at the back, looking over the finances. Ginger Scoops isn't doing terribly, but not as well as I'd like. People come in, they enjoy my ice cream, occasionally there are busy spells...but we're getting into summer, and I'd hoped to be doing a little better by now.

I have Instagram, Facebook, and Twitter accounts for Ginger

Scoops and post semi-regularly. We also have a website. We've had a few small-time food bloggers write about us, but we haven't gotten big press.

This is a crucial time and I need to focus on making sure my business succeeds, yet I'm starting a new relationship. Is that really such a great idea?

I imagine flipping the sign on the door from "open" to "closed" for the very last time, and I press my fists to my eyes to prevent the tears from falling.

I *have* to make this work.

"Chloe?"

It's Drew.

"Valerie let me in," he explains.

I look at the time. It's nine thirty.

"Are you okay?" he asks.

"I'm fine. Just looking over the books." I shake my head. "Our sales numbers need to be higher. I assume you aren't an expert in marketing?"

"Marketing." He makes a face, and I can't help but laugh. "You have a good product. You haven't been open that long. It'll work out."

"Look at you, Mr. Optimistic."

"Well, you do make a good product."

"First of all," I say, "you only tried it once, and that wasn't exactly a raging success."

"Everyone else loves it."

"Second of all, lots of restaurants make good food and don't survive. A good product is only part of it."

"I believe in you."

"Have you turned into Havarti Sparkles?" I joke.

However, he sounds like he truly means it, and I don't think Drew is the sort to throw statements like that around carelessly.

He pulls me up from my chair and gives me a hug. "Come

home with me. You've been here since eleven thirty, haven't you?"

I nod.

"Did you eat dinner?"

"No."

"You have to take care of yourself. You can't think clearly on an empty stomach."

We go to his place, and he lifts me onto a stool at the breakfast bar in his kitchen.

"How about a grilled cheese?" he says. "Cheddar is the only cheese I have. Is that okay? I'll put some basil in it, too. That's how I like it."

"Sounds good."

Drew slices several pieces of cheddar and places them on top of a piece of bread with basil leaves. Although it's not very exciting to watch someone make a grilled cheese sandwich, I love looking at him as he moves around the room, his intense concentration, the bulge of his arm muscles.

I love that he's taking care of me. It's not something I'm used to anymore.

While the sandwich is cooking, he cuts up some carrot and celery sticks for me. This makes me melt more than anything, the fact that he's making sure I get my veggies.

"Would you like your grilled cheese sliced in two?" he asks.

"Diagonally, please."

"Not horizontally?"

"What are you, a monster?"

"Shh." He puts a finger to his lips. "I don't want word to get out."

"That's okay. I like you anyway."

He smiles as he cuts my sandwich, then places the plate of grilled cheese and vegetables in front of me. "Eat up."

Drew is a little surly on the outside, but he's complete mush inside.

How did his ex not see that?

Afterward, he lets me raid his chocolate stash and massages my shoulders. We sit on the couch together, arms around each other.

I could stay here forever.

But that's a dangerous thought. I can't lose my focus; I can't afford to jeopardize my business. I started Ginger Scoops in honor of my mother, and I have to prove to my father that I wasn't crazy to give up my goal of being a dentist.

For tonight, though, I can let Drew be a distraction. I climb onto his lap and kiss him, really kiss him. His arms are around me, his hands slipping through my hair, and it feels so good. So right.

In fact, I'm hit with the overwhelming feeling that I *belong*.

I DIDN'T LOOK after Michelle last weekend, but I've decided to see her—and the rest of my family—more often going forward. I like spending time with my niece.

When I get to Nathan and Adrienne's house that Saturday, Michelle rushes to greet me at the door. "Uncle Drew!"

"Hey, Michelle." I smile.

"We're going to use the pasta maker together. We're making fettucine with mushrooms!"

"Sure, sweetie."

Nathan appears. He came back from Seattle for good last weekend. "Just going out to run an errand."

"You have to come back for lunch, Daddy. Uncle Drew and I are cooking for you."

"Don't worry, I'll be here."

Michelle and I head to the kitchen. On the table, there's a long list of pasta shapes in her handwriting, as well as the long list of cheeses she made the other week.

"Mommy said you don't know how to spell mozzarella," she says.

"She's right. I don't."

"It's M-O-Z-Z-A-R-E-L-L-A."

Michelle spells it three more times to make sure I've learned my lesson—yep, I'm being schooled by a six-year-old—before we get out the flour, eggs, and salt. Since she's made pasta with her father twice already, she's the expert, and she keeps bossing me around.

"I think we're done," I say after I've kneaded the dough for five minutes.

She glares at me. "It's not done. It has to be smooth and elastic, Uncle Drew. It's not smooth yet. The recipe says eight to ten minutes."

She has the whole recipe memorized, apparently. I can't help marveling at her memory.

Finally, Michelle decrees that the dough is ready and it's time to let it sit for thirty minutes.

"How about ten minutes?" I say, just to annoy her.

"No! It has to be thirty minutes!"

I laugh. "Okay. Thirty minutes. What should we do while we wait?"

"We're going to make an arugula salad."

"Sure."

"And a ten-layer chocolate cake!"

I give her a look. "You're being silly."

She can't stop giggling. "How did you know?"

"Because it takes more than thirty minutes to bake a ten-layer chocolate cake."

I tickle her, and she continues to giggle.

"Do you think Chloe can teach me how to make ice cream?" she asks.

"You can ask her the next time you see her."

Michelle jumps up and down. "I'm going to make ice cream!"

"Wait until you ask her."

But I'm sure Chloe will say yes, and I get some warm, fuzzy feelings at the thought of them in the kitchen together.

"Chloe is my hero," she says.

"I thought the rat in *Ratatouille* was your hero."

She shakes her head. "Chloe is real, not a cartoon, and she's prettier than a rat—"

"I'll be sure to tell her you said that. Such a big compliment."

"—and she makes ice cream for her job! Isn't that cool?"

"Well, she's my girlfriend, so obviously I think she's pretty great. But I wish you hadn't told your mother about our date. You did not hold up your end of the deal, Michelle," I say with faux sternness.

"I couldn't help it. It was really exciting news!"

She takes some vegetables out of the fridge, and we spend the next half hour preparing the salad and cutting up the ingredients for the pasta sauce. We work mostly in silence, aside from when Michelle is telling me what to do, but my mind is anything but silent.

I can't stop thinking about how heartbroken Michelle would be if Chloe and I broke up.

I also can't help thinking about how I'll never get to spend time in the kitchen with my own children.

After all, millions of people have read the line that said I would make a horrible father, and the person who wrote that book was in the best position to judge.

I have no intention of subjecting a child to a horrible father.

Suddenly, my eyes are watering, even though I'm not cutting onions.

After I have lunch with Nathan and Michelle, the three of us play board games for a while before I head back downtown, planning to have a bottle of beer and a few squares of chocolate while I read on my balcony.

Then I remember that I finished my thriller last night and I don't have anything to read. So after getting off the subway, I walk to the big bookstore nearby and find a few books in the mystery and suspense section. Books that promise dead bodies and creepy villains, and probably don't contain unicorns or ice cream.

But because of Chloe, I want to learn to like ice cream. I'm determined to do so. Maybe if I lick it off her naked body...

I file this idea away for later and head to the checkout on the first floor. However, it's crazy busy on the first floor. Perhaps there's some kind of event.

And then I see the sign:

3-5 pm: Book Signing with Lisa Mathieson, Author of Embrace Your Inner Ice Cream Sandwich.

Oh, God.

I look around. There are crowds of people holding a familiar teal book with an ice cream sandwich on the cover. Mostly middle-aged white women, but there are other people here, too. I make my way toward the signing table set up at the far end of the store. I can't get too close, however, because the line-up is super long. I can just barely make out Lisa, sitting at the table.

I knock into another sign and turn to see an enormous close-up of an ice cream sandwich. The sight is nearly enough to make me gag. The sign is so large that the raisins in the cookies are practically the size of my fist, and the ice cream looks so damn creamy...

I hurry toward the exit, then pause.

Although I don't need a signed copy of the book, I do have something I want to ask Lisa, and she's probably done lots of signings and is very efficient at them by now.

Sure, the line is long, but it can't be more than ten minutes, right?

Wrong.

Half an hour later, I'm still standing in line, and I have a splitting headache.

"At first I thought my ice cream sandwich was chocolate chip cookies and vanilla ice cream," says one of the women behind me, "but then I realized I wasn't being true to myself. I wasn't accepting my quirky side; I was always stuck in the same old patterns. So I went to an ice cream shop near my house, Fancy Schmancy Ice Cream, every day for a month and tried all the flavors. I realized my inner ice cream sandwich isn't plain vanilla but pear-vanilla-peppercorn inside a ginger-molasses cookie, and my asshole of a husband had denied my true nature and turned me into plain vanilla ice cream. That's when I knew I had to get divorced. Now, I always keep a pint of pear-vanilla-peppercorn ice cream in my freezer, and I make sure my cook keeps my pantry stocked with ginger cookies."

Oh my God. I want to punch something.

"Well, *my* inner ice cream sandwich is dark chocolate ice cream inside lemon-rosemary shortbread cookies, and let me tell you, Ricky is very good at respecting it."

Pear Vanilla Peppercorn sighs. "You're so lucky."

"But I think my aura is black cherry ice cream."

What?

I try to push this conversation out of my mind by focusing on the women in front of me. There are three of them, about my age.

"I wish I had the money to travel around the world like Lisa Mathieson," one woman says. "I don't, but at least I have the money to buy myself an ice cream every now and then. It's important to treat yourself, you know? Women shouldn't need a self-help book to tell them that, but that's the problem with our society. Women are expected to think of everyone but themselves."

"This is fucking ridiculous," says one of her friends. "We finally found an afternoon when we're all free to hang out, and what are we doing? Standing in line at a book signing for some pretentious self-help writer I'd never heard of until today. Why are we here when we could be pouring wine down our throats? Someone better buy me a fucking drink for putting up with this."

"I'll buy you an ice cream sandwich instead," says the first woman. "Actually, I'll buy you something even better. A bubble waffle with a double scoop of ice cream. There's this great place nearby called Ginger Scoops..."

My ears perk up.

"...They have so many great flavors. The ginger and matcha cheesecake are amazing, but my favorite is the strawberry-lychee sorbet. I've decided my inner ice cream sandwich is oatmeal chocolate chip cookies with strawberry-lychee sorbet. I'm a rebel —instead of an inner ice cream sandwich, I have an inner sorbet sandwich! Wait, that doesn't sound nearly as cool."

"My inner ice cream sandwich is chocolate cookies and mint chocolate chip ice cream," says the third woman, "and I will protect it at all costs."

"What the fuck is wrong with you two?" asks the second woman, who I am now calling Fucking Ridiculous. "Inner ice cream sandwiches? Will you listen to yourselves?"

"Maybe you should read the book before you judge," says Strawberry Lychee.

Ugh. Why is this line-up taking so long? I consider leaving, but I've already wasted more than half an hour. I'm not going to give up yet, even if my patience is hanging by a thread.

"Her ex-fiancé sounds like a giant dick," says Mint Chocolate Chip. "Good thing she climbed out that church window."

I stiffen.

"And then she went on an expensive trip around the world to find herself?" says Fucking Ridiculous. "Is she aware of how much privilege she has? That poor guy is lucky to be rid of her."

"Marvin Wong is not a good guy," says Strawberry Lychee. "Trust me, I read the book three times. I know how the story goes."

"You read the book *three times?*" Fucking Ridiculous stares at her incredulously, as though the idea is...fucking ridiculous.

"Hey! It's a good book. Anyway, Marvin Wong..."

I don't want to hear complete strangers discuss my failings. I'd read one of the thrillers in my hand if I could, but it's just too damn loud in here to concentrate.

Instead, I listen to the scintillating conversation of Pear Vanilla Peppercorn and Cherry Aura.

"I'm pretty sure my dog's inner ice cream sandwich is spumoni ice cream with peanut butter cookies," says Cherry Aura.

For fuck's sake. Waiting in this line is worse than my nightmares about unicorns. If I ever talk about my dog's inner ice cream sandwich—not that I have a dog—I hope someone hits me over the head with a two-by-four.

I'm getting closer to the signing table, closer to Lisa. My heart is thumping. I'm worried about how she'll answer my question.

Chloe, I tell myself. *Remember Chloe.*

She's the reason I need to know the truth.

"My inner ice cream sandwich is wine," says Fucking Ridiculous.

"Your inner ice cream sandwich can't be *wine*," says Mint Chocolate Chip.

At least they've stopped talking about me, and they're not talking about the inner ice cream sandwiches of their pets, either. Though frankly, it wouldn't surprise me if someone mentioned their budgie's inner ice cream sandwich right about now.

I glance at the signing table. I have a good view of Lisa from here. She's wearing a navy blazer and a colorful scarf, and her blonde hair falls in soft waves. She looks good, I admit. However, I feel nothing when I look at her. No surge of affection, like I might have experienced once upon a time.

Okay, that's not quite true. I *do* feel something.

Annoyance.

Now that I'm nearing the front of the line, I can see why it's taking so long. Lisa is attempting to have a conversation with everyone who comes to get her autograph. She's probably asking them about their inner ice cream sandwiches and listening to stories of how the book changed their lives. Some sort of nonsense like that.

"It's almost our turn!" says Strawberry Lychee excitedly.

"Does anyone have any wine?" asks Fucking Ridiculous.

"I wish," I mutter.

I would prefer a bourbon barrel-aged imperial stout, but wine would do.

"Do you think Lisa Mathieson will want to hear about Pixie Dust's inner ice cream sandwich?" asks Cherry Aura. "Should I get Pixie Dust her own signed copy?"

"You probably don't need to get a book for your dog," says Pear Vanilla Peppercorn. "I can't believe we're actually here! It's so exciting."

Definitely not the word I'd use.

It's now Strawberry Lychee's turn. She briefly tells Lisa about how she loved the book, then gets a signed copy and asks for a photo. Lisa obliges.

Mint Chocolate Chip is next. Fucking Ridiculous, in a move that doesn't surprise me at all, doesn't ask Lisa for her autograph.

I step up to the table.

"What's your..." Lisa trails off when she sees who it is. "Marvin...I mean Drew."

Suddenly, the crowd of women is quiet. Strawberry Lychee, Fucking Ridiculous, and Mint Chocolate Chip were walking away, but they turn back to look at me.

And then everyone starts talking.

"It's Marvin Wong!"

"How can it be Marvin Wong? He wouldn't dare show his face at one of her signings."

"But she said 'Marvin'! He looks Chinese, and he's about the right age. It must be him."

"I don't know, I think he's Korean."

"OMG. He looks like Chris Pang."

"Who the hell is Chris Pang?"

"I bet he's here to ruin her signing."

"It's Marvin Wong!"

"Marvin Wong!"

"It's that asshole she almost married!"

I turn away from Lisa and look at the crowd. There are lots of angry women. And then they start advancing on me like a landslide. I'm jostled from behind.

"Drew," Lisa hisses. "Get behind the table. Quickly."

I follow her instructions, unable to think for myself.

There must be over a hundred women here, and they all look like they want to clonk me over the head with their purses. They've read the book. They think I'm the monster who crushed the spirit of their beloved heroine.

"Security!" Lisa shouts. "Everyone, please, stop this."

I hurry away from the table and duck behind a bookshelf, but Cherry Aura and Pear Vanilla Peppercorn find me.

"You don't deserve to escape," says Cherry Aura.

"What are you going to do? Set Pixie Dust on me?" I retort.

"I bet your inner ice cream sandwich is dog shit between two slices of moldy bread."

"Why are you such a huge asshole, Marvin?" asks Pear Vanilla Peppercorn.

Someone grabs my arm, and I flinch.

"Come with me," says Fucking Ridiculous.

A security guard joins us while another security guard attempts to calm the swelling crowd. I'm led out an emergency exit and onto the street. I bend over, hands on my knees, and rapidly breathe in the fresh air.

"You okay?" asks Fucking Ridiculous.

"Uh…yeah." I can't manage any more words.

The security guard nods, seeming satisfied that he's done his job.

Fucking Ridiculous cocks her head to the side. "Actually, you're kind of cute. You look like Chris Pang. You want my number?"

"I've already got a girlfriend," I say.

"I assume she isn't obsessed with a stupid book about finding your inner ice cream sandwich."

"No, but she runs an ice cream shop. Ginger Scoops, the one your friend mentioned."

Fucking Ridiculous throws her head back and laughs. "I bet most of the shit in that book is false. Why were you at the signing?"

I don't answer that question, just shake my head. It was clearly a mistake to waste forty-five minutes of life waiting in line, only to have a mob of women rush at me before I could talk to Lisa.

"Thanks for the help," I say. "I better get out of here before they find me."

I start jogging home.

Once I'm in my condo, I make myself a strong coffee and sit on the balcony.

I caused a mini riot. *Me.*

A normal man wouldn't cause an angry mob of women to descend on him like that. A normal man wouldn't be ripped apart in an international bestseller. A normal man would at least like ice cream.

I am not a normal man.

I didn't need to ask Lisa my question after all. I already knew the truth; I just didn't want to admit it.

I might not be Lisa Mathieson's biggest fan, but she managed to write a book that really spoke to millions of people around the world—that's no small feat. Lisa is a decent person. There's a reason we were together for four years; there's a reason I proposed to her. Even when her fans turned on me, she tried to get me out safely.

Lisa wasn't lying in her book. She was right about me.

I think of Chloe.

It's like a fist clamping my heart.

Chloe is a joyful, generous person who's thrown everything she has into a business that makes people happy. Whereas I snuffed out someone's spark, inspiring her to go on a journey of self-discovery to "find herself" because she'd lost herself when she was with me.

The thought of that happening to Chloe is just too damn painful. She might not think I could do that to her now, but I haven't been with her for long. She doesn't know me like Lisa does.

If I truly love Chloe…

Wait a second. Do I love her?

Yes.

I love Chloe Jenkins.

And because I love her, I have to walk away. I want her to be happy, and I don't see how she can be happy with me. Maybe in the short term, but not in the long term. If she wants to have a family—and I'm pretty sure she does—I want her to have one. But I can't provide that for her. I should not have children if I'm going to be a crappy parent who would crush their dreams.

Before, I told myself that Lisa was exaggerating, but after the events of today, I can't think that anymore. I know, in my bones, that she's right.

I don't want to break up with Chloe, the only woman I've loved in a long, long time.

But I'm going to do it anyway.

She deserves a better boyfriend than me.

SUNDAY AFTERNOON, Grandma and Dad walk into Ginger Scoops.

"Grandma, you were just here on Tuesday!" I say.

She waves this away. "What's the point in living to eighty if you don't get to do whatever you want? If I want to go out for ice cream twice in a week, then I will." She turns to my father. "You have to try the durian."

My father dutifully takes the sample I offer him. "This smells revolting." He tastes it. "No, not for me."

"Try the green tea," Grandma says.

"I had it last time. I don't think tea belongs in ice cream."

Grandma rolls her eyes. "I will have the durian, green tea, and Vietnamese coffee in a medium cup."

"And I will have chocolate-raspberry and ginger," Dad says.

"Come sit with us when you have a minute, Chloe," Grandma says as I scoop out her ice cream. "I have a question for you."

I serve the next family in line, then leave Valerie to deal with the customers while I sit with my family.

"What's your question?" I ask my grandmother.

"I want to try durian. The fruit, not the ice cream. Where can I get one?"

"It's, uh, rather expensive, and very smelly,"

"I know how it smells."

"You shouldn't bring it into your house. Maybe you could start by trying the frozen stuff in a package. You can get it at T&T, I think."

"What's T&T?"

"It's an Asian supermarket," Dad says. "I can take you, if you like."

I sit there as my white father and grandmother make plans to go to an Asian grocery store in the suburbs, which isn't something I'd ever expected to see.

My grandmother reaches into her purse. "I have something for you," she says to me, then pulls out a copy of *Embrace Your Inner Ice Cream Sandwich*.

I stifle a laugh.

"I read it last week," she says. "We're going to discuss it at our next book club meeting. It's actually quite good."

"It sounds like a bunch of baloney," Dad says.

She continues on. "I think my inner ice cream sandwich is chocolate chip cookies with durian and green tea ice cream inside."

"Are you allowed to pick two flavors or is that against the rules?" Dad mutters.

"There are no *rules*."

"Your inner ice cream sandwich stinks, quite literally."

"John!" She proceeds to lecture him as though he's a schoolboy.

When they're ready to leave, Dad turns to me and says, "You're still coming over for dinner tomorrow, right?"

"I'll be there."

Monday night, I'm at my father's, and rather than barbecuing, he's heating up a frozen lasagna and making a salad, which reminds me of the dinner Drew cooked for me. I suppress a smile as he sets a plate in front of me.

I haven't seen Drew in a few days. I texted him yesterday and asked if I could come over after work. It took him a while to respond, and then he said something vague about having plans.

Hopefully I can see him tonight. I miss him.

Dad and I chat about work. I ask about his cases and half-listen as he drones on about stuff that doesn't interest me. But I don't mind, because that means he isn't badgering me about my career choices.

You know what? I'm going to have it out with him once and for all. It wasn't the right time when Anita visited, but it is now.

"Dad." I put down my fork. "I need you to stop nagging me to finish university and apply to dental school. Every time I see you, I worry you're going to bring it up again, and I try to distract you with other topics in the hopes you'll forget about it. But I'm tired of this. I want to see you without having to worry you'll criticize my career choice."

He looks at me for a moment, then down at his plate, then back up at me. "You could do better than what you're doing now. I just want you to do the best you can. It's like you don't believe in yourself anymore."

Is he serious? "That's not true. In fact, going against what was expected of me? Taking a leap of faith and opening my own business? That required me to have a lot of faith in myself." I don't voice my fear that maybe that faith was misplaced, maybe my business will fail because we aren't getting enough customers. I'm worried, yes, but I'm determined to do everything I can to make it succeed. "I realized what I wanted to do with my life, and I made it happen."

"But what you wanted was to go to dental school."

"Dreams change."

He shakes his head. He can't accept that my dream has

changed from something he approved of to something he doesn't approve of at all.

"This is my choice," I say. "Stop trying to get me to do something else. Don't you want me to be happy?"

"You won't be happy like this, not in the long run. You think it's all fun and games to run an ice cream shop—"

"I don't think it's all fun and games! It's a lot of work, and I spent years preparing for this. Learning about the business, taking courses. I only have one day off a week now."

"Still. It's frivolous."

I've said that about myself before, but it's different when it comes from my father.

It hurts.

"Stop it." I look down at my lasagna and stab it with my fork.

"Stop acting like a child," he shoots back. "You work in an ice cream shop. You painted it pink, for God's sake. Pink with unicorns, like you're six."

"Because it makes me happy! And it's an ice cream parlor. It's supposed to appeal to kids. Besides, what's wrong with the color pink? Are feminine things inherently bad?"

"You think you're so different because you have flavors like green tea and durian."

Ugh.

"No, I don't. There are other places like that, and people like them—even Grandma does, and you know how she's all about Jell-O salad and butterscotch." I swallow. "It's for Mom, you know. She used to take me out for ice cream, and she loved the ginger ice cream at that place in The Beaches, hence the name."

He stares at me.

"You told me..." My voice wobbles. "You told me that you never thought of Mom as Chinese, and it's haunted me ever since. You act like she was white, but she wasn't. You're denying her family history. You're denying how people treated her differently because of how she looked."

"We should all be treated equally," he says gruffly.

"But we're not. There are racist assholes, even in a diverse city like Toronto. And you want to deny where her family came from? That was a part of her, Dad, and it's a part of me."

He doesn't say anything.

"Sometimes, I don't know what to do about it because my mother is dead and I don't speak the language and I can't even really cook the food. I *am* Chinese Canadian, but I feel like a fraud when I call myself that. So, okay, maybe some of those ice cream flavors are a frivolous—as you say —way of expressing my heritage, of reconciling my Chinese-Canadian identity when I'm not first or second generation, but you don't understand that I have to deal with any of this."

I take a deep breath. I'm finally getting it all out, these words I've thought of saying to my father for so long.

"You think we should just deny that race exists," I say, "but I can't. That's a luxury only white people have, and you can't seem to get it through your head that I'm not white. I *don't* look just like you."

"But you're my daughter, and nothing changes that. Why are you bringing this up?"

"You don't have to understand all of it, but can't you accept that this affects me? Like, people regularly ask me where I'm from, and when I say 'Canada,' they get annoyed." I glance at the lasagna on my plate. I have no appetite. "I'm not unhappy with who I am, even if it's difficult at times and I feel like I don't belong anywhere. But *you're* unhappy with who I am—"

"I never said that."

"—and I don't feel like I belong when I'm with you, either. My career choice isn't good enough for you, and I'm not white like you seem to think. You want me to force myself in a box, and I don't fit into it."

"Chloe..."

My dad is looking at me as though I'm a deranged alien. Like he has no idea who I am.

And he doesn't.

It hurts so much that he feels that way, because he's the only parent I have left, because I love him, despite feeling misunderstood whenever I'm around him.

I often felt misunderstood by my mother when I was a teenager, but I think, when it came to the big things, she understood me.

Or maybe I'm wrong. Maybe I've edited my memories of her without realizing it.

"You think you're progressive because you married my mother," I say, "but it's still easy for you to be ignorant of so many things. You don't understand me at all, like I'm an outsider in my own family." Tears well up in my eyes, but I hold them back because he probably thinks tears are childish, like unicorns.

He sighs. "I love you. You know that."

"Then why haven't you tried to understand me?"

"You're being unfair."

I want him to tell me he'll do better in the future. Maybe ask me to clarify one of the many things I said to him. Something like that.

But it's clear he's not going to say anything close to what I need him to say.

I get up from the table. "I'm leaving."

He sighs again, exasperated. "You don't need to leave."

But I do.

I get off the streetcar and start walking home, but then I change my mind.

I want to see Drew. He'll listen. He'll understand. He'll make me feel like I belong.

When he opens the door to his unit, he smiles, but that smile quickly fades and his eyes fill with concern. "Darling, what's wrong?"

I was crying silently on the streetcar. I must look awful right now.

He folds me in his arms, and we stand there for a long time. I feel a tiny bit better with each passing moment. There's something wonderful about his hugs. I feel safe enough to shed a few more tears, and then he leads me to the couch.

"You were having dinner with your dad tonight, right? What happened?" He pulls me into his lap.

I tell him about my fight with my father.

"Is it stupid?" I ask him. "That my ice cream store is, in a way, me trying to connect with my heritage? Me trying to find some kind of third-generation Chinese-Canadian identity?"

He shakes his head. "Nothing about you is stupid."

Just that simple reassurance is nice. When I'm with him, I feel accepted for who I am. I don't feel too white, or too Asian, or too frivolous. Drew is, in many ways, the opposite of me, yet I think he sees me for who I really am, and he loves me for it.

Yes, I think he loves me.

And I love him.

I didn't know it until this moment, but I do.

I squeeze him against me and kiss his mouth desperately.

"Chloe," he groans as I run my hand over his abs. "I…"

"What?"

"Never mind," he mutters, and then he's pulling my shirt over my head and unhooking my bra.

I pull off his shirt, too, and we both groan as his skin meets mine. His hands roam all over me, up and down my back, over my breasts. When he grazes my nipple, it's enough to make me gasp. He pulls my nipple into his mouth and scrapes his teeth over it, and God, he feels so good. I thrust my hands through his hair and rock against his erection.

I need to feel him inside me. So badly.

I fumble with his button and zipper and wrap my hand around his cock. He's satiny and hard, so hard for me.

"Drew. Please."

He slides his hand inside my jeans and panties and runs his finger over my slit.

Fuck. It's good, but it makes me crave him even more.

Thankfully, he shoves down my pants and underwear, then picks me up and sets me on my feet beside the couch.

"Bend over the arm of the couch," he says roughly. "I'll be right back. Going to get a condom."

The air is cool against my bare skin, against the moisture between my legs. My nipples tighten as I wait for him to return and make me feel complete.

There's the crinkle of a foil wrapper, and then he's rubbing the tip of his cock over me.

"Please," I beg. I don't care how desperate I sound. I need him.

Instead of entering me, he toys with my clit as he bends down and licks between my legs. He pleasures me with his tongue, and my whole body tenses before I cry out for him.

"Drew!"

"Yes, darling, it's me."

He stands up and holds me through my orgasm, then rubs himself against my entrance again before thrusting inside.

It feels so good. It feels so right.

He grasps my ass as he pumps into me, over and over, and it's so intense, but I love every second. We're together. Joined.

It's rough but intimate. Not only does he have me naked, but he sees me. Really sees me.

He leans over and grabs one of my breasts while his other hand dips between my legs. He touches my clit, and that's enough for me to come apart again in his arms. He thrusts into me a few more times before he stiffens and comes with a growl.

I smile; I love doing this to him.

Afterward, we lie tangled together on the couch. We put on our underwear, but we're otherwise naked.

Though my life isn't perfect, I feel like I can handle anything right now. Normally, I shy away from expressing difficult emotions. But with Drew in my life, I know everything's going to be okay. It was silly to think I'd lose my focus because of him, which is what I told Sarah about Josh; there's no reason to avoid a relationship right now.

I need to listen to my own advice.

Josh is perfect for Sarah, and Drew...

I hug him close and whisper, "You're perfect for me."

[22]
DREW

YOU'RE PERFECT FOR ME.

For one moment, I'm elated.

You're perfect for me, too, I want to say. *I love you so much.*

And then I remember.

I was supposed to break up with Chloe.

But when she arrived, tears in her eyes, I couldn't turn her away. I listened; I comforted her. That's what everything in me demanded I do. I hate it when she's upset, and I'm pissed at her father. Why doesn't he see what a wonderful woman she's become?

Instead of breaking up with Chloe, I held her, and we had sex. I thought it would be less intimate if she was bent over the sofa, if I couldn't see her face.

But it was Chloe, and so it was still intimate.

Now, though, I have to do the right thing. The timing is crap, but I can't let this continue.

I abruptly sit up and pull on my T-shirt. "You're wrong. I'm not perfect for you—in fact, I'm no good for you at all—and we can't keep doing this. We have to break up."

She frowns. "I don't understand. If you feel that way, then explain the past half hour."

"I'm an asshole, and I wanted to fuck you one last time," I say, deliberately crude, wanting to push her away.

"Before the sex—how do you explain that?"

I clench my hair in frustration. "You just have to accept that I'm not the man for you."

"Drew, I think—"

"It's over, sweetheart. We don't belong together."

Her face crumples. It utterly crumples, and I'm the one who did that.

"I love you," she whispers.

No, don't say that! She's making this so difficult.

"You don't really love me," I say, desperately needing that to be true. I know how painful it is to be dumped by someone you love, and I don't want her to hurt too much. "You don't know what you're talking about."

Her eyes flash. "How dare you say that? How dare you say I don't know my own feelings? I'm not a stupid little girl. You're acting like my father, thinking you know what's best for me." Her voice is a little angry, but more than anything, it's full of dejection.

I flinch. I'm not like her father. I don't want to impose my dreams on her. I don't deny who she truly is.

But breaking up is for the best, and she'll realize that eventually.

"Let's be honest," I say. "We haven't known each other all that long. You might think you know me, but you don't."

"I *do* know you," she whispers.

"No."

Her lower lip trembles. I reach out and press my thumb to it, but she shifts away and stands up, shaking her head. She puts on her pants and T-shirt and grabs her purse.

She's going to leave, and I'm never going to see her again. The thought is an unbearable ache in the pit of my stomach.

Well, maybe I'll see her if Michelle insists on going to Ginger Scoops, because if my niece wants to go there, I wouldn't say no. But otherwise, I won't see Chloe again.

This is for the best. I have to keep telling myself that. I'm doing this for her.

I'm doing this because I love her, even if I didn't say the words.

I would crush her spirit, and I would be a terrible dad to her children, and she doesn't deserve any of that. She deserves a better person than me.

She steps out the door without another word.

A funny thing happens after Chloe leaves.

I go to my chocolate stash because I deserve some good chocolate after doing the right thing, don't I?

Except I'm not simply craving chocolate.

No, for some inexplicable reason, I'm craving chocolate *ice cream.*

I walk to the grocery store and buy some dark chocolate ice cream, the good stuff that I used to enjoy. Then I sit on my balcony with the pint and a spoon and shovel ice cream into my mouth. It's actually pretty good, and it doesn't make me gag.

How times have changed.

After eating too much of it, I text Glenn to see if he'd be up for a few drinks this week, and then I attempt to forget about Chloe by reading a book about grisly murders.

But nothing can make me forget her.

WE DON'T BELONG TOGETHER.

If his goal was to hurt me, that was the perfect thing to say.

Before, he made me feel like I belonged for once, but I guess I was wrong.

I shouldn't have been so stupid and put my heart on the line. For years, I had sex and half-heartedly attempted relationships, but I didn't really put myself out there, didn't open up to anyone. And then I did, and for a brief period of time, it was everything.

I should have known better.

And I should have known better than to think telling my father the truth would change anything. Now our relationship will be strained, and he's the only close family I have left.

I stagger down the street, not knowing what to do with myself. I could visit Valerie, but I don't feel like it. I feel so alone right now, and for some reason, I think seeing a friend would just heighten that feeling. Plus, I'm not really in the mood to talk, and when I'm not in the mood to talk, Drew is the only one who can make me feel better, but...

We're over.

I don't belong with anyone.

In the end, I decide to go home. I live in a house with three other people, but I don't know them very well. We pass each other in the halls, bump into each other in the kitchen, occasionally make small talk, but I can't say we're friends.

Still, I go home. I head up to my bedroom and cry quietly so no one will hear.

~

Not surprisingly, I don't sleep well that night. Thoughts of Drew keep running through my mind. I remember the day he first walked into Ginger Scoops with Michelle, the time he came in during a rainstorm and kissed me…

God, I want it to stop.

I want my mom.

I want her to hold me and tell me everything will be okay.

But she's gone.

She's been gone since I was twenty. The night she died, we had a stupid argument about my messy room and the fact that I didn't come home until three in the morning that Saturday. I told her I was an adult, in university; she said if I lived at home, I had to follow her rules.

I love you.

That's what I should have told her instead.

My life has formed around her absence. A giant void opened up in my world, and everything changed because of it. I imagine a boulder suddenly appearing under a tree, and how all the roots would have to grow around it. My life would be completely different if she were still here, but I try not to dwell on it. It's not worth thinking about what might have been.

But I do think about how it would feel to have her comforting me.

Some people say everything happens for a reason, but I don't like thinking that my mother's death in a car accident happened for a reason. To me, that's a horrible thought.

It just…happened. It was senseless.

I get up at six o'clock in the morning after two hours of sleep and take the subway to the north end of the city. My mother is buried in the same cemetery as my grandparents, but in a different section. There's a little creek, flowerbeds, and a large tree near her grave. Dad paid extra for that spot.

What if last night was the last time I'll ever see my father alive? I didn't tell him I loved him. I didn't even eat the dinner he'd made for me.

I sit on my mother's grave, arms around my knees. There's no one else here. Just me and the quiet sounds of the creek and the birds. The sky is already a bright blue, and it seems wrong that it's such a lovely shade of blue on a day like today.

Sometimes nothing makes sense. That's just the way it is.

I remember when my first girlfriend dumped me. I'd met her during frosh week at university, and we had a few months together before she broke up with me over the Christmas holidays. I hadn't seen it coming.

Mom held me as I cried, and later, we went out for ice cream. I felt like a little girl again, but it was nice. I managed a few wobbly smiles because I knew that I would always have her, I would always be her little girl, she would always take care of me.

And maybe, from some distant place, she *is* taking care of me— I don't know what to believe about death. But even if she is, she can't put her arms around me, she can't take me out for ice cream, she can't tell me I'll find another person to love and it'll all be okay.

Instead, I'm sitting on her grave.

I sob.

Usually when I go to the cemetery—a few times a year—I feel numb. I don't cry at all. But something has opened up inside me, and now I feel too much.

I want my mother.

I also want Drew, but if my mother had lived, I may never have met him.

This is why it's best not to think about what might have been.

I hug my knees to my chest, trying to substitute for the touch of another person, but it's not the same. It's nowhere near the same.

I am alone.

~

The rest of the week is a blur.

I go to work. I obsessively straighten the tables and napkins. I make a new batch of passionfruit ice cream. Valerie asks me if something's wrong, but I force a smile and say, "Nothing."

I don't think she buys it.

On Saturday morning before Ginger Scoops opens, I have a Skype date with my aunt and her new family. I'm doing it at the ice cream parlor so they can see what it looks like. Anita and two little girls appear on the screen.

One of them waves at me. "You're our new cousin! Chloe, right?"

I nod. "And you are?"

"Keisha!" She bounces in my aunt's lap. "I can't believe you work in an ice cream shop! My other cousins are babies. They don't do much other than cry. They don't work in ice cream shops. Mommy says it's really good ice cream!"

I walk to the counter with my tablet and show them the tubs of ice cream. Keisha asks me about each one. Sasha doesn't say much but watches intently. She's apparently the quiet one and spends lots of time with her books. She also likes drawing.

"Which ice cream would you want to try, Sasha?" I ask.

She twists her mouth, as though thinking very hard. "Chocolate-raspberry."

"Good choice."

"I want to try all of them!" Keisha says. "Especially the purple one."

"Taro," I say. "That's a good choice, too."

Sasha crosses her arms. "They can't *all* be good choices. I bet the purple one is nasty."

"You're wrong!" Keisha pushes her sister.

A minor kerfuffle ensues, but my aunt soon gets everything straightened out, and I show them the unicorn in the corner and the patio out front. Keisha decides to name the unicorn Twinkle.

A few minutes later, I talk to Isaac and Deidre, and then Aunt Anita returns.

My mother would have been thrilled for her. If Mom were still alive, I bet Anita would have told us about her girlfriend and invited us to the wedding, even if it was a small affair.

"So, what's new with you?" Anita asks.

I don't want to talk about me. "How was the rest of your honeymoon?"

She tells me a little about Montreal and Quebec City but quickly turns the conversation back to me. "What's wrong, Chloe?"

"Nothing's wrong."

She gives me a look.

"Mom would have been very happy for you."

Her smile is sad. "I know."

I hesitate. "Drew broke up with me, and I had a fight with my father. So, to be honest, things aren't great, but somehow, I'll make it through."

"I know you will."

I don't feel like telling her the details, but it's good to know she's back in my life and plans to stay there. She says she'll call me next week.

If Aunt Anita and I can have an argument and then come out stronger on the other side, then maybe that will happen with Dad and me, too. But it's a different situation. I was angry at my aunt, but ultimately, we wanted the same things. She showed up in Toronto already wanting to make a change.

My father, however, hasn't called me since our argument, and I've been doubting myself. Whenever the phone rings, I keep expecting it to be him, but it never is. Perhaps I shouldn't have made such a big deal about everything? After all, I don't have it that bad.

Still, it had been haunting me for so long.

I blow out a breath. I'm not sure how it will turn out with my dad, but I don't think I regret telling him the truth. It had to be done.

Valerie and I arrive at Sarah's at seven thirty on Sunday evening. Sarah immediately pushes me into a chair, shoves a glass of wine in my direction, and hands me a meat pie.

I down most of my wine in one gulp, and Valerie and Sarah exchange a look.

"Okay, work week's over," Valerie says, "and you've had some wine. *Now* will you tell us what happened?"

"Why do you think something happened?" I ask, playing innocent.

She rolls her eyes. "Oh, for fuck's sake. You haven't been yourself all week. You've got bags under your eyes, and you aren't talking much, and your smile looks forced. And Drew hasn't come by Ginger Scoops. Did you break up?"

I nod before shoveling meat pie into my mouth.

"Well?" Valerie demands. "I need some details. Did he end it?"

I nod again.

"That bastard. Tell me where he lives and I'll—"

"Val." I sigh. "Stop it. There's no need for any of that. I expressed my feelings for him, and he told me we don't belong together." My voice hitches on the last two words. "I thought he felt the same way about me, but I was wrong."

"I guess that idiotic book was right after all. He's an asshole. Like most men."

"No, *Embrace Your Inner Ice Cream Sandwich* is a load of garbage. The way Lisa Mathieson told it, he wasn't supportive at all and he held her back, but that's not the guy I know."

"You don't need to defend him," Valerie says. "He's your ex. Besides, the man hates ice cream. That's not natural."

"But he wasn't melting my inner ice cream sandwich!" I can't believe I said those words. I eat some more pie and drink some more wine. I'm starving. I forgot to eat lunch today. "We like very different things, but he made me stronger rather than holding me back. Really, he did."

I can't reconcile the Drew I know with the Drew—well, Marvin Wong—in Lisa Mathieson's book. Has he changed over the past few years? Is she lying? Is he a lot different with me than he was with her—and why?

Drew feared that his ex was correct about him, but I know, in my heart, that she's not correct about him being a crappy boyfriend, at least not anymore. But perhaps that's why he ended it, saying he wasn't right for me. He truly thinks he's no good for me because of what she said.

I shake my head. No, I'm pretty sure he just didn't want me but was trying to be kind.

"More wine," Valerie says to Sarah. "She needs more wine so she can forget about that fucking asshole."

Sarah fills my glass with white wine, then hands me a piece of chocolate tart with Vietnamese coffee ice cream.

"Chocolate," I whisper. "He loves chocolate. He has a chocolate stash in his kitchen, did I tell you that?" I shove the plate away.

Yeah, he's ruined chocolate for me. I bet that's temporary, but it's upsetting nonetheless.

"Shit," Valerie says. "This is serious. You sure you don't want to tell me where he lives?"

Sarah puts another pie dish in front of me—a quarter of a lemon-lime tart—then squeezes the top of my shoulder, near my neck. Like Mom used to do.

I've been holding in my tears since I came back from the cemetery on Tuesday, but now, I let them fall.

"I miss my mother," I sob. "I had a fight with my father because he's still pushing me to go into dentistry. He can't accept that I have no interest in it anymore, and he can't accept that I'm…never mind. It's stupid."

"I bet it's not." Sarah hauls me to my feet, and she and Valerie support me as they lead me to the couch. Valerie returns to the kitchen to get the lemon-lime tart and our wineglasses, and then my friends each sit on either side of me.

Valerie was my best friend before my mom died, and she's still my best friend now, but there's a distance between us that wasn't there before. Losing my mother was an isolating experience, not only because I lost such an important person in my life, but because it set me apart from all my friends, who still had two parents.

One minute my mother was there, and the next she was gone. She died instantly, which I guess was for the best—I hate to think of her lingering in agony—but I never got to say goodbye.

That gulf between me and other people was partly my own doing. It was my way of surviving, and that's exactly what I did. Being cheerful in public, but not opening myself up further, helped me cope.

I *am* a happy, peppy person, and people expect that of me, and I *like* being that person, but being with Drew was like permission to not have to act that way when I wasn't in the mood. He made me feel safe.

Most of the things I tell my friends, while I drink my wine

and stuff my face with dessert, are things I've already told Drew. It's not so hard now.

These are my friends, and I belong with them, too.

And it's okay to feel what I feel. It's been a few years now, and I no longer have to keep everything bottled up in an attempt to manage my grief.

By ten o'clock, I'm drunk, high on sugar, and all cried out. I've said everything I need to say, and I feel…well, pretty crappy, to be honest, but a part of me feels at peace.

"I miss Drew so much," I whisper. "I still don't really understand what happened. We were so good together, and then…"

"It's okay," Sarah says soothingly. "Sometimes these things just happen."

"I really want to kick that idiot's ass," Valerie grumbles. "If only you'd let me."

"Did you see his arms?" I certainly spent a lot of time admiring them. "He would have no trouble defending himself from the likes of you."

"Then I'll force him to eat ice cream."

That makes me laugh, really laugh. I feel unhinged, crying one moment and laughing the next.

I try to stand up, but my legs aren't working right.

"Do you want to spend the night here?" Sarah asks.

"Sure." It's only a twenty-minute walk home, but that sounds impossible right now.

Valerie decides to stay, too, so we pull out the couch to turn it into a bed, and Sarah gets us some blankets.

I fall asleep as soon as my head hits the pillow.

I open an eye, then immediately shut it.

The room is too bright. Why is it so bright?

And why is someone snoring next to me?

Drew!

Yes, it must be Drew.

I've never heard him snore before, but it's a light snore, not loud enough to shake the marbles in my brain. How I've missed him.

I throw an arm over the other side of the bed, and to my surprise, encounter a breast.

"Chloe!" shrieks someone who is definitely not Drew.

Valerie. Right. The events of last night slowly come back to me.

I'm at Sarah's, on her pull-out couch, and Valerie is next to me

"Sorry," I mumble, opening my eyes. "I thought you were Drew." I sit up. My back hurts—the couch probably wasn't the best place to sleep—and my head hurts, too. Is that from the booze or the crying? I fumble for my purse and pull out some ibuprofen. I'm about to swallow it dry, but Sarah appears with some orange juice.

"What the hell is Havarti Sparkles?" Valerie asks. "You kept mumbling that in your sleep."

"It's the unicorn Drew painted at his niece's paint-your-own-unicorn party."

"Right."

"I'm sorry I tried to snuggle you. I didn't mean to grope your breast."

"It's okay. We're cool."

Valerie and I sound like shit, but Sarah is perky.

"Breakfast?" she asks. "I can make blueberry pancakes and bacon. Coffee?"

"Sounds good," I say.

As Sarah sets about cooking breakfast, I check my phone. To my surprise, I have texts from an unknown number, as well as several missed calls. All from this morning.

First message: *Dear Chloe, I have gotten a smart phone. Now I can be cool and text! Love, Grandma.*

Second message: *Dear Chloe, Sorry, I accidentally pocket dialed you four times. Love, Grandma.*

Third message: *Lillian informs me that I don't need to say "Dear Chloe" and "Love Grandma" in every message. I don't know. It seems impolite to me.*

Fourth message: *Here is my first selfie!*

There is not, however, a picture of my grandmother, but one of the carpet.

Fifth message: *Sorry, that didn't work. Here is my first selfie!*

This message is accompanied by a picture of half my grandmother's face.

Sixth message: *I hear these emojis are cool.*

This is followed by the eggplant, peach, and poop emojis.

I stare at the screen, eyes wide, unable to make a sound.

Seventh message: *Do you think that last emoji is supposed to be soft-serve chocolate ice cream?*

"What's going on?" Valerie asks. "You look horrified."

"My grandmother learned how to text." I hand Valerie my phone.

As she scrolls past the eggplant and peach emojis and bursts into laughter, I'm reminded of the present Drew gave me. The eggplant and peach amigurumi, which are sitting on my night-table at home. I feel like someone is clenching my heart and squeezing too hard, just at the thought of an eggplant and a peach.

Ugh. This is ridiculous.

"Chloe? Did you see the video your grandmother sent you?"

"She sent me a video?"

"Well, it took her four attempts, but..."

Valerie holds the phone between us. Grandma's text says: *You know that ice cream sandwich book I gave you? Apparently the author did a signing in Toronto last week.*

There's a link to a jerky video taken on a phone. Valerie turns on the sound, and I hear someone shout, "Marvin Wong! It's

Marvin Wong!" A crowd of women rush toward a man standing by a table.

It's Drew.

Drew was nearly trampled at one of Lisa Mathieson's signings. And if this was last week, maybe it explains everything.

"What was he doing at that signing?" Valerie asks.

"I don't know."

"Maybe he wants her back?"

I glare at my friend. "She left him at the altar and trashed him in a book. I don't think so. If I had to guess, I would say he wanted answers." I replay the video. "I bet this is why he broke up with me. Being mobbed by a group of angry women made him think that the book was correct, and he started to truly believe he didn't deserve to be with me. I thought he didn't share my feelings and was trying to let me down easy, but—"

"Chloe." Valerie looks at me sadly. "You have to move on. It's over."

Sarah comes over with our cups of coffee. "I don't know. Chloe might have a point. Drew's situation is rather unusual, and some things deserve a second chance."

"Absolutely not." Valerie is probably thinking about her ex.

My friends continue to argue about second chances, and I sip my coffee and stare at my phone. Should I visit Drew? Ask him exactly what happened with Lisa?

Or should I just move on?

I can't stop myself from sending him a text, a simple *Hey, how are you?*

An hour later, he hasn't responded.

But my grandmother has texted me again: *My boyfriend has informed me that I should not have sent you the eggplant and peach emojis. When he told me what they mean, I was mortified. I've also learned that the other emoji is not actually chocolate ice cream...*

Wait a second. My grandmother has a boyfriend?

GLENN IS busy with his family, so it's another week before we're able to meet at the bar. I sit sullenly at a table in the back, imperial stout in hand, as I wait for him.

It's been a shitty week. I haven't slept well, and I had another dream—I refuse to call it a nightmare—about unicorns. Also, a colleague stole my chocolate at work again, and it took every bit of restraint I had not to yell at him.

I've spent most of my free time at home, moping and thinking about Chloe. About how it felt to wake up with her pressed against my chest, about the way her laugh made me smile. I remember eating dinner with our hands clasped together under the table. I want more of that, but I can't. I can't do that to her.

And after a year of not being able to eat ice cream, I've finished two pints in a week.

A video of me being chased out of the bookstore has gone viral, and it's racked up millions of views and thousands of comments on YouTube. Some people have commented on my resemblance to Chris Pang, and there's even a petition to cast Chris Pang as Marvin Wong in the movie adaptation of *Embrace Your Inner Ice Cream Sandwich*. There's also wide speculation about why I was at the book signing. Some people suspect I was trying to win Lisa back; others think I was there to give her a piece of my mind. One weirdo thought I was trying to warn her of an impending alien attack.

A Korean-American journalist used the video as a starting point for his rant about how tough Asian men have it in the dating world. Of me, he said, "This guy has it all. A good job, good looks, a full head of hair, and rather than chasing after him for a date, women are trying to run him out of a bookstore." Actually, that video spurred a number of discussions about race, which I've done my best to avoid, though I did see a post by someone who complained that my bad reputation was making things even worse for Asian men in the dating world.

"Hey, Drew." Glenn sits down across from me. "I saw the video."

"You and everyone else in the world," I mutter.

"Is that why you look like trash?"

"Do I?" I say mildly. "I hadn't noticed."

He gives me a look.

"I had a break-up."

"I didn't know you were seeing anyone. I thought you weren't dating anymore."

"I wasn't, but Chloe…she was special."

"You want to talk about it?"

I shake my head. "But I was wondering if you could ask Radhika to do me a favor."

"Sure, man. What is it?"

"Chloe owns an ice cream shop on Baldwin Street. Home-made ice cream, Asian-inspired flavors. Taro, Vietnamese coffee, Hong Kong milk tea ice cream—things like that. It opened a few months ago, and business is not as great as it could be. I was wondering if Radhika could review it on her blog?"

Radhika is a fairly well-known Toronto food blogger, and if

she gave Ginger Scoops a good review, I think it would make a difference for Chloe.

I only want the best for her, and the best isn't me.

Glenn regards me for a minute. "Are you trying to win her back?"

"No, I'm the one who ended the relationship, but I still want to do this for her."

"Why did you end it?"

I open my mouth to tell him the truth. That I'm no good as a boyfriend. For anyone, but especially for Chloe, who is such a sweet and lovely person—I couldn't bear the thought of changing her. I don't want another woman to have to go on a long journey of self-discovery because of me.

I shrug. "Just didn't work out, you know? But I want her business to succeed."

"I can't believe you dated someone who owns an ice cream shop."

"I can't believe it, either."

"I'll talk to Radhika and see what I can do."

Saturday morning, I'm drinking a cup of black coffee and scowling at the sunlight coming through my window when my phone rings.

"Buzz me up!" shouts Adrienne.

I have no idea why Adrienne is here, but I let her in.

A few minute later, my entire family comes through my door. Mom, Dad, Adrienne, Nathan, and Michelle.

Oh, for fuck's sake.

"You want to visit my girlfriend again?" I snap. "Well, she's not my girlfriend anymore."

"I knew it." Mom turns to my father. "Didn't I tell you? You thought he was being anti-social because of the video, but I knew it was more than that."

Dad claps me on the back. "Good to see you're alive. You look like crap."

"What on earth is going on here?" I demand.

"Nobody had heard from you in a while," Adrienne says. "Not even a text message."

"Then why didn't you call?"

"I did call, but you didn't answer."

Hmph. That's entirely possible.

"We were worried," Adrienne continues. "We wanted to make sure you were okay, especially after we saw that altercation on YouTube."

"Wait!" Michelle says. "Uncle Drew, did you say Chloe isn't your girlfriend anymore? You broke up?"

"Yes."

"But Chloe's my hero!" Michelle sounds tearful.

God, I'm making my little niece cry. I'm a monster.

Well, I already knew that.

"You can still go to Ginger Scoops and see her," I say.

Michelle glares at me. Despite her short stature, it's a terrifying glare. "Why did you break up with her? What did she do wrong?"

"She did nothing wrong."

"Why were you at that silly woman's book signing?" Mom asks. "What good did you think that would do? Or are you still not over Lisa? She left you at the altar and wrote a book about it. What's wrong with you?"

"Don't worry, I'm over Lisa."

"I don't understand what happened. I liked Chloe."

"You didn't like that she runs an ice cream shop and doesn't have a university degree."

"Maybe I was too harsh on her."

I raise my eyebrows.

"I don't know," Mom says. "She seemed nice."

"Wow, what a ringing endorsement." My voice drips with sarcasm.

"I know what happened," Adrienne says.

"Please, enlighten, us." Dad sits on the couch, hands behind his head. "Because I frankly have no idea."

My sister crosses her arms and walks around me in a circle. "Drew, you see, has a rather fragile male ego."

"What's a fragile male ego?" Michelle asks.

Adrienne ignores her and jabs her finger into my chest, "You read *Embrace Your Inner Ice Cream Sandwich* recently, didn't you?"

I nod.

"When you went to Lisa's signing, you wanted answers. You wanted to know why she wrote that stuff about you. You wanted to know if it was all true. But you didn't get to ask your question because you were run out of the room by a bunch of angry women, and you took that as your answer—that you don't deserve love."

I roll my eyes. "Who made you a psychologist?"

"Aiyah!" Mom looks at me. "Is she right? I can't believe this. What's wrong with you?" She hits my shoulder. "One woman didn't appreciate you, and now you think that's it?"

"That woman left me at the altar and wrote a book that sold millions of copies in twenty-three languages."

"Oh, cut it with the twenty-three languages crap," Adrienne says.

Mom throws up her arms. "Did I raise you to be such a *wuss?*" She turns to my father. "This is your fault."

"I'm not a wuss," I protest. "I just…I didn't want to…" God, how to say this? "I didn't want to melt another woman's inner ice cream sandwich."

"You mean by leaving it out in the sun?" Michelle asks.

I chuckle. "No, not like that."

"That book is a load of crap," Mom says. "Why are you

quoting it?"

"It helped a lot of people," I mutter.

"Those people are idiots! I did not raise my son to listen to such bullshit!"

"You said the S-word!" Michelle says.

"Okay, this is getting out of hand." Adrienne turns to my parents, then Nathan. "Why don't you all go to the playground with Michelle? I'll stay here with Drew. I don't think the big family intervention is working."

Mom grumbles, but she leaves with Dad, Nathan, and Michelle. I make some more coffee for Adrienne, and we sit at the table together.

My older sister looks at me like I'm a pathetic creature. "So, you think you're being noble by letting Chloe go?"

"Something like that."

She sighs and shakes her head. "You think she's better off without you, but I don't believe that. You love each other—"

"Who said that?"

"I just know."

"What, you have some kind of sixth sense?"

"Stop being an ass. I understand Lisa's book got to you, but aside from being an annoying little brother—"

"Thanks."

"—you're a good person, and Chloe would be lucky to have you. I don't know if Lisa's talk about you stifling her spirit was complete bullshit or just mostly bullshit, but I doubt most people feel that way about you, even if you're a bit of a grump. I mean, that's not what you're like with my daughter. You always encourage her interests."

I do. I've even been looking up recipes to make with Michelle and ensuring I know how to spell any pasta shapes and cheeses she might think of.

Adrienne has a sip of coffee. "I'm not sure exactly what happened with Lisa, but you shouldn't assume that what she said applies to all your relationships. That woman's not the brightest crayon in the box. She climbed out a window when there was a perfectly good door *right there*."

I let out a long sigh and scrub my hands over my face. "I'll think about it."

"By the way, would you be able to babysit Michelle tomorrow for a few hours? Nathan and I want to spend some time together alone, now that he's back from Seattle."

"Alright," I say, "but we're not going to Ginger Scoops."

∽

Sunday afternoon, Michelle and I are walking down Queen Street, heading to a ramen restaurant she wants to try.

"It's supposed to be really good, Uncle Drew." As she skips along beside me, she recites some facts about miso that are surprising to hear from a six-year-old, but that's Michelle.

I'm in a weird mood. I couldn't sleep well again last night. I kept thinking about my family's visit, about what Adrienne said.

I'm still not sure about any of it, but I admit it might be possible for me to be with Chloe, though the "he would make a horrible father" line in the book still haunts me.

Michelle stops skipping and points at a window. "Look! It's Colonel Mozzarella."

I'm so confused right now. "Who's Colonel Mozzarella?"

"The alpaca you got me for my birthday. I named him Colonel Mozzarella."

I realize we're standing in front of Libby's Gifts, and there's an alpaca, like the one I bought Michelle, in the window.

Michelle jumps up and down and points at something else. "It's a unicorn suit." She giggles. "You should try it on."

There is indeed a mannequin wearing a unicorn onesie. It's mostly blue, though the chest is white. There's also a hood, featuring little ears, a pink mane, and a goddamn yellow horn.

It is the most horrifying thing I have ever seen in my life.

Yet I smile because it makes me think of Chloe.

My niece grabs my hand and drags me toward the door. I could resist her if I wanted to, of course, but I let myself be dragged inside. She insists that I ask the store clerk if the unicorn suit comes in children's sizes, preferably in the color purple.

It's a no on both counts.

Michelle frowns, but then she jumps up and down again. "Please try on the adult one, Uncle Drew!" She goes to the rack of unicorn onesies at the back and picks one up. "It's perfect for you."

I put my hands on my hips. "Why do you think it's perfect for me?"

"It matches your eyes."

I stare at her.

"That's what Mommy said about the last shirt she bought for Daddy!"

"Right."

Michelle clasps her hands together. "Please?"

I look into my niece's pleading eyes and think, *What the hell? Why not?*

I head to the store's only change room, unicorn onesie in hand. It's pretty loose, and I'm able to pull it on top of my clothes once I take off my shoes.

I admire myself in the mirror.

Well, "admire" is the wrong word, but you get the idea.

To my horror, I discover that in addition to the ears and the horn and the mane, the unicorn onesie has a pink tail.

Sullenly, I pull back the curtain to the change room, and Michelle shrieks when she sees me, then doubles over in laughter. "You're a unicorn!"

I do unenthusiastic jazz hands. Or hooves.

"We need to take a picture," she says. "Where's your phone?"

Great. Just what I need. Photographic evidence.

But whatever, I'll do it for my niece. Besides, millions of people have already watched an embarrassing video of me, so what does it matter at this point?

I had the phone over to Michelle, who doesn't need any help taking a picture.

"Smile!" she says. "Unicorns should always be smiling."

I manage a smile.

To my surprise, it's a genuine smile. I'm not going to buy the unicorn onesie, and I desperately hope there are no other customers in the store, but I don't mind embarrassing myself if it makes my niece laugh.

Michelle takes a couple pictures, then says she wants to be in the photos, too. The store clerk is happy to oblige. I pick Michelle up in my arms, and he takes a picture.

After I remove the unicorn onesie, I tell Michelle that I'll buy her an amigurumi—I'd feel bad about asking the store clerk to take pictures if we didn't buy anything—and my niece, unsurprisingly, picks a unicorn. I see a peach amigurumi, like the one I gave to Chloe, and my heart twists.

For fuck's sake.

I can't get that woman out of my brain.

On impulse, I select an ice cream cone amigurumi, then go to the cash register to pay. We then proceed to the ramen restaurant, and fortunately, we don't pass any more stores with stuffed alpacas, unicorn onesies, or similar.

The ramen restaurant was featured on Glenn's wife's blog, *Radhika in the 6ix*. (Frankly, I think calling Toronto "the 6ix" is beyond stupid, but somehow it caught on.) It's quite busy, and the only table available is a high top. I boost Michelle into the chair and sit across from her. She puts her unicorn amigurumi on the table.

"What are you going to name him?"

She glares at me. "It's a her."

"Right. Of course it is. Because it's pink."

"No, not because it's pink, but because I decided. It's a her."

"Okay."

"She's named Miso Glitter!"

"Hello, Miso Glitter, are you going to join us for ramen?"

Michelle giggles, and my heart twists again.

I want this. With my own son or daughter, and I no longer believe I'd make a horrible father. I tried on a freaking unicorn onesie for my niece. I would do whatever it takes to be a good dad.

Yesterday, I started wondering if I was wrong to break up with Chloe, and now, something unclenches in my chest.

There's no reason I can't have a future with her. I know I can be a good boyfriend, too. If she still wants me, that is.

My phone beeps and I pick it up.

Adrienne: *lol lol lol*

Apparently Michelle sent one of the unicorn onesie pictures to her mom.

There's another text message, too. It's not from someone on my contact list, but I recognize the number.

Lisa.

I wait for Lisa at a Starbucks not far from my condo.

I'm not in a great mood. Adrienne and Nathan picked Michelle up an hour ago, and I'd rather spend this time trying to figure out how to get Chloe back, but instead, I've agreed to meet my ex-fiancée.

Five minutes later, Lisa Mathieson sits down across from me with a grande Frappuccino. I wonder if she's planning a sequel to her bestseller. *Embrace Your Inner Frappuccino.*

I hide a smile.

"Drew." She sweeps an assessing gaze over me. "How are you?"

I shrug. "I'm alright."

"I want to apologize for what happened. I'm so sorry. Calling you 'Marvin' at the bookstore was an honest mistake."

"I know."

"I had no idea it would inspire a rampage."

"I know."

"Or that the video would get millions of views on YouTube."

"I know."

"Though perhaps I should have expected it. My life's been pretty crazy for the past year."

"I know."

She tilts her head to the side. "Do you know any other words?"

"I accept your apology."

I can't believe I once planned to marry this woman. She's pretty, and she carries herself with more poise than she used to.

But she doesn't do anything for me now.

I swallow. "Did you mean everything you wrote about me in your book?"

I don't need answers from Lisa, not anymore, but she wanted to meet up, and I thought it might provide closure. I'm curious to know why she wrote what she did.

"I meant it at the time," she says slowly, "but in the two years since I wrote the book, I've come to see that I exaggerated. *I* was the main reason I wasn't in touch with my inner ice cream sandwich. I shouldn't have blamed you for melting it."

Ugh. I really hate the idea of an inner ice cream sandwich. It's ridiculous.

"I don't regret breaking up with you, though," she says. "You and I never quite clicked. But I do regret the way I left you on the day of the wedding. I had doubts before, and I should have talked to someone about it, called the wedding off beforehand. I hope you've found someone else."

"Sort of. It's a long story. I couldn't bear to think of dating again after what happened, and then I did, but..." I pause. "Do you really think I'd make a terrible father?"

"Did I say that in the book?"

The one line that haunted me, and she doesn't even remember it's there.

"I mean, I remember thinking it," she says hurriedly, "but I don't remember putting it in."

"And why did you think that?"

"You were so uncomfortable with Michelle when she was a baby and a toddler. You didn't know how to talk to her, how to play with her. But I understand now. My father says he was like that, too. He'd never been around babies before I was born, but he learned, and I think he was a great dad. Plus, there was also..." She looks away.

"What?"

"My mother thought you'd be a super-strict Tiger Dad and—"

"Oh, for fuck's sake. Just because I'm Asian?"

"I know, I know, but for some reason, that got in my head. God, Drew. I'm sorry. I didn't really think about how the book would affect you. Are you afraid to have children because of what I said?"

I look away. "Not anymore, but I was."

"Shit," she says quietly. "Shit. The book was meant to inspire people to change their lives and get out of a rut. I didn't mean to do the opposite to you. Many women stay in relationships that don't do anything for them. I stand by the message of the book, even if it seems hokey to you. Embracing your inner ice cream sandwich *is* a good approach to life."

Oh, it does seem hokey to me, but I understand.

"But some of the details aren't quite true. The 'Marvin Wong' I put in the book—that's not how I think of you now, and I do think you'd be a good father and husband, if that's what you want. Some men *are* total turds, but you and I just weren't right for each other."

Yes, that's really what it comes down to. Lisa may be a bit clueless at times, but she's the one who figured out what needed to be done. Not me.

"I was so caught up in the idea of getting married before I was thirty," she says, "that I didn't really think about whether it was for the best. I was too focused on that goal, and it was holding me back from being true to myself. Until the day we were supposed to tie the knot, and I realized what I was doing."

I blow out a breath. "Well, I'm glad you did, even if the goddamn cookies in your inner ice cream sandwich have raisins, of all things."

She chuckles. "How's your family? Michelle must be five or six now."

"She just turned six."

"Do you have a picture?"

I pull out my phone, then realize the last picture I have of my niece is from Libby's Gifts. When I was wearing a unicorn onesie.

Whatever.

I hold out my phone, displaying a picture of me in the unicorn onesie, carrying Michelle.

Lisa bursts into laughter. "Can I use this as a picture of Marvin Wong in my next book?"

I give her a dark look.

"You never would have done this for me," she says. "Put on a unicorn onesie for my amusement, I mean."

"Yeah, well. There are only two people in the world who could make me do that." I put my phone down. "Actually, could you do something for me?"

She nods. "I owe you."

"The woman I was seeing owns an ice cream shop."

Lisa laughs once more.

"Yeah, yeah, it's hilarious. Anyway, she could use some publicity, and you're, well..." I gesture vaguely. "Your name is now synonymous with ice cream."

"Does she make ice cream sandwiches?"

I shake my head. "She does bubble waffles, though."

"Maybe I could do a blog post about her?"

"Yeah, something like that, maybe. I don't know." Most of Lisa's readership isn't near Toronto, but I figure enough of them are that it might make a difference.

"Okay." She touches my wrist before standing up. "I hope you find your inner ice cream sandwich, Drew."

Before I can reply, she's gone.

～

I go home and read the Marvin Wong chapter again, now that I have a different perspective.

Lisa described me as grumpy and dour...and yes, that's true sometimes. It's who I am, and that's okay—not everyone needs to be a freaking ray of sunshine. It doesn't make me bad at relationships. She needed a different kind of guy, though, whereas Chloe and I have very different personalities, but we play off each other in a positive way.

Chloe helps me be a better person, and I will do everything I can to support her.

I'm no longer bothered by what the book says. If people want to hate me, they can hate me, but I know I'm good for the people who are most important to me, and that's what matters most.

And really, *Embrace Your Inner Ice Cream Sandwich* is about how the life you envision for yourself isn't necessarily the one you need; it's about figuring out who you really are.

That's not a terrible message, even if it's wrapped in some pretty cheesy packaging.

I close the book.

Time to make a plan to get Chloe Jenkins back.

I'M HYPERVENTILATING.

Earlier, Lisa Mathieson was in Ginger Scoops—I recognized her from her author photo. She ordered a sugar cone with Vietnamese coffee and ginger ice cream, then took a number of pictures with her phone. I wonder if she's going to say something on social media about my store. A part of me hopes she'll change her inner ice cream sandwich from mocha to ginger ice cream, but somehow, I doubt that's going to happen.

And now, Radhika in the 6ix is here! I recognize her face from her food blog, which is one of the biggest in Toronto. She's here with a man who's pushing a toddler in a stroller.

God, I hope she likes my ice cream. That would be amazing for my business.

"Very cute store," she says.

"Thank you."

"I'd like to try the matcha cheesecake."

My hand shakes as I hand her the spoon. She tilts her head to the side after she tries it, then smiles. "That's amazing. I've never had anything like it before."

"Th-thank you."

"You're Chloe, the owner, right?"

I nod.

She introduces herself, asks me a few questions, and takes a picture of me standing behind the counter. She also tries a few more samples before ordering a waffle cone with matcha cheesecake and Hong Kong milk tea.

"How did you hear about us?" I ask as I make the bubble waffle.

"My husband is friends with Drew."

Oh. I understand now.

Drew must have asked both Radhika and Lisa to come to Ginger Scoops. I feel a strange pressure in my chest.

I hand Radhika her order, and she tells me she'll have her review up tomorrow.

~

"Your grandmother has a boyfriend," my father says.

"I know," I say, cutting off a piece of my grilled chicken. "She mentioned him in a text message."

"Has she been texting you, too?"

"Yes. She sent me a bunch of inappropriate emojis."

He laughs, but it sounds brittle.

It's Monday night. Dad invited me over for dinner, and I didn't say no. Because he's my father, and we've hardly talked in the past couple weeks, and I miss him. I'm glad he finally called, but he hasn't brought up our argument yet, and our conversation is a bit tense, even as we talk about inconsequential things like emojis. I can't help feeling anxious about where our relationship will go from here.

"Her boyfriend is Vietnamese," Dad says. "Came here in the seventies. He's eight years younger than her."

"A younger man. How scandalous!"

Dad laughs again, but then his expression turns serious.

Okay, here we go.

"I've been thinking about what you said," he begins. "I've been thinking about it a lot, actually. First of all, about dental school. The reason I wanted so badly for you to go was because I refused to accept that your mother's death had changed you, like it changed me. I wanted you to want the same things you did before. Like...proof it hadn't completely altered the direction of your life. I was clinging to the past."

I nod. I get it.

"But, unfortunately," he continues, looking away from me, "she's not here anymore, and I have to accept the effect it's had on our family. You're different now, and that's...okay." His voice wobbles. I reach across the table and squeeze his hand. "So I won't bother you about it, not anymore, when it's clear you have no interest in it."

"Thank you."

"She would have been proud of you."

I swallow. I know she would have been proud, and it's nice to hear my dad say it to me.

"About...the other things. I thought ignoring your race—and your mother's—was the best way to move beyond the racism we see in the world, but I was erasing our differences rather than accepting and celebrating them." He pauses. "I do know that people treated her differently because of how she looked. You also have to understand that your mother didn't like to talk about these things. She was brought up in a different time, in a part of Toronto that was very white back then, and felt a lot of pressure to be just like everyone else. The world around her told her that she should hate who she was, and she often resented her background and felt ashamed of it. So, I know it might sound strange to you, but she might have even liked it if I said 'I never saw you as Chinese.' To her, it might have meant 'I see you as a person, not just how you look different from me.' But now, I understand how what I said is problematic."

Oh. Thinking back… My mother would buy a tin of mooncakes for the Mid-Autumn Festival and give me a red envelope at Chinese New Year, but that was it. She didn't talk about these things with me, either. I wish she had. I wish she'd passed more on to me, but I get it now.

I hate that she was made to feel ashamed of who she was.

"So that's where I'm coming from," Dad says. "And it's why your mother insisted you grow up in a diverse neighborhood, so you wouldn't have her experience. When you weren't teased at school for how you look—like she was—I guess I thought your race just wasn't something we'd need to talk about. But I've been doing some reading, and I recognize there were problems in the way I looked at the world, at my own wife and daughter. Of course the world still sees you differently than me. And I'm glad you aren't embarrassed by her family's background and want more connection to it." He squeezes my hand. "I promise to do better in the future. I can't promise to be perfect, but I will do my best to understand. I see you, Chloe. I won't continue to ignore what you say. I'm sorry."

"Thank you," I whisper.

I want so badly for us to have a good relationship. For years, I couldn't bear to tell him how I was really feeling, afraid it would harm our relationship further, but now, I feel like I don't have to hide everything from him for us to get along.

"How's your boyfriend?" He's trying to change the conversation to an easier topic, but…

"Drew isn't my boyfriend anymore," I say, "but I hope we can work things out."

I know Drew sent Radhika and Lisa to Ginger Scoops. He's thinking about me.

Maybe he'll come back to me.

Maybe, if I still haven't heard from him in a few days, I'll go to him.

"I want to clarify something," I say to my father. "Even though I had a boyfriend, that doesn't mean I'm straight."

"I understand that."

"When I was twelve, after I had that conversation about bisexuality with Mom, I heard the two of you talking. You told her that she shouldn't encourage me to define myself that way, not when I was so young."

"I remember. She talked me out of it."

"Once she was gone, I felt like nobody understood me."

He smiles sadly. "We'll be okay, Chloe, even if it's not the life I'd imagined for us. I said she would be proud of you, but I want you to know that I'm proud of you, too. For everything you are."

"Thank you," I manage, my voice rough.

Before I leave that evening, he gives me a long, long hug.

It might not be perfect between us, but he's listening to me and accepting the choices I've made, and it's a good start. And he's helped me understand my mother better, too.

If only she were here to have these conversations with us.

Radhika hadn't published her review when I got to my dad's—I checked obsessively all day—and I refrained from looking at my phone while I was there. But as soon as I leave his house, I pull it out of my purse.

Unlike usual, I have dozens of notifications for my Ginger Scoops Twitter account.

Radhika has put up her post, *Ginger Scoops: The Hot New Ice Cream Shop in Town*, with a picture of her bubble waffle and ice cream, and the picture of me at the counter. She has lovely things to say about it.

Lisa has also put up a blog post and tweeted about my ice cream shop. *Torontonians: Haven't found the perfect ice cream for your inner ice cream sandwich? Try one of the inventive flavors at Ginger Scoops in Baldwin Village.*

I roll my eyes, but OMG.

OMG.

People are actually talking about Ginger Scoops!

I run back into my dad's house. I'm talking a mile a minute, and I'm not sure how Dad can understand what I'm saying, but he does. He grins and hugs me again, and I do a little dance, not ashamed to be who I am in front of him.

Ginger Scoops is busy on Tuesday. No line-ups out the door, but Tuesday is usually a slow day, and there are twice as many customers as usual. I'm busy scooping ice cream and making bubble waffles and ringing up orders—and realizing I need to make a new batch of matcha cheesecake ASAP. I'm so busy that I don't even have time to think about Drew.

Ha. No. That's a lie.

I think about him all day, wishing I could feel his strong arms around me once more, his skin against mine.

I'm different because of him. Before, I'd been coping, going through the motions and working toward the life I wanted but struggling to connect with people.

Now, because of Drew—a man I once compared to Oscar the Grouch—I've changed. It started with me opening up to him, but now I feel like I can do that with my friends and family, too. I can allow myself to really feel the emotions I used to keep locked in a box, and it's okay.

I am me, and I think I'm pretty awesome.

It's almost nine o'clock in the evening now, and I'm heading to the door to change the sign from "open" to "closed" when my phone buzzes.

Grandma: *Lillian says you're very popular on something called Twitter?*

Grandma: *My boyfriend (tee-hee, I have a boyfriend!) got me a selfie stick so I can take better selfies now. Here is a picture of us.*

In the photo, they're sitting at a table with a platter of deviled eggs and a bowl of lime Jell-O salad. Some things never change.

But other things do, thank God.

Sarah walks in. "You're closed now. Time for you to come with me."

I stare at her in confusion. "I have to clean up."

"I'll do it." Valerie steps out from behind the counter.

"Where are we going?" I ask as Sarah tugs me out of Ginger Scoops.

She shrugs, a smile on her face.

"Tell me!"

"You'll see soon enough."

Interestingly, we're walking in the direction of Drew's building, and indeed, that's where Sarah comes to a stop. She buzzes him and says, "We're here."

The door clicks, and she holds it open for me.

Drew wants to see me. I'm hopeful, but afraid to get too excited.

Sarah winks and walks back into the night, and I head to the elevator. My heart hammers as I walk down the hallway to his unit. When I knock on the door, he opens it immediately.

"You're here," he says.

"I'm here."

We look at each other for a moment.

"Close your eyes," he murmurs.

I follow his instructions, and he leads me through the condo and out the door to his balcony. He helps me into a chair.

"Now open them," he says.

I do.

On the little table in front of me is the biggest sundae I've ever seen. There are several scoops of ice cream in a large glass bowl, and I'm pretty sure they're flavors from Ginger Scoops: ginger, Vietnamese coffee, taro, and green tea. There's also a generous amount of whipped cream. The whole thing is drizzled with strawberry sauce and chocolate sauce and topped with chocolate shavings, maraschino cherries, and rainbow sprinkles.

It looks amazing.

It looks like the sort of thing Drew wouldn't touch with a ten-foot pole, and yet there are two spoons.

He gets down on his knees and takes my hands in his. It's wonderful to feel his touch again, to see the serious expression on his face. It's wonderful just to be with him.

"I screwed up," he says. "I'm so sorry. I let my insecurities get the best of me. I let myself believe that everything in the book was correct, and I could never be a good boyfriend for anyone, but that's not true. I might be the man who got chased out of a bookstore—"

"I saw the video."

"I figured." He clears his throat. "But I'm also the man who's perfect for you. You were right about that. I love you, Chloe, and I've put my insecurities behind me. I'm a better, happier version of myself when I'm with you, and I promise I will always be there for you, whatever you need. We can do it together."

He looks up at me earnestly.

I love him so much.

And he loves me.

"You're an amazing woman," he says, "who has turned my life upside down. A few months ago, I never would have imagined making a huge ice cream sundae. I never would have imagined wanting another serious relationship with a woman—and feeling like I was capable of it. But things have changed, thanks to you, and I want you to be an important part of my life." He squeezes my hands. "You're perfect for me, too. Please say it's not too late. Will you take me back?"

I nod, unable to form words, and bend down to kiss him.

His kiss is exquisite, and it promises so much more, but right now…

"We should eat the sundae before it melts," I say. "Is the ice cream from Ginger Scoops?"

"Yes. Valerie got it for me."

"But you still don't like ice cream, do you?"

"I started craving it after I broke up with you. Believe it or not, I'm looking forward to eating this."

He sits on the chair beside me, then lifts a spoonful of Vietnamese coffee ice cream, whipped cream, chocolate sauce, and strawberry sauce to my lips.

It's the most delicious thing I've tasted in my life, and that's partly because I'm with Drew. Plus, I make pretty great ice cream, if I do say so myself.

I scoop up some ginger ice cream and chocolate sauce and feed it to him. He even licks his lips afterward.

Wow. He really has changed.

"Michelle says you're her hero," he says, "and wants you to teach her how to make ice cream."

"I will."

"You'll never guess what she got me to do the other day."

He pulls out his phone and shows me a photo. It takes me a few seconds to make sense of it, but when I realize what it is, I can't help bursting into laughter.

It's Drew in a unicorn onesie.

OMG, it's Drew dressed up as a unicorn.

I have to put my spoon down because I'm laughing too hard.

We're together now, and everything is going to be more than okay. And when it's not, I'll just look at this photo and it'll make me smile.

We eat our ice cream in silence for a few minutes, occasionally feeding each other bites. Then we share a kiss that tastes of ice cream and chocolate, and he presses his cool lips to my cheek.

"Thank you for asking Radhika and Lisa to come to Ginger Scoops," I say. "We were twice as busy as usual today."

"It wouldn't have happened if they didn't like your ice cream. It's because of you that you were so busy today, and because of you that I know Ginger Scoops will be a success."

He has so much faith in me.

I know I can do it.

"Lisa invited me out for coffee," he says. "She wanted to apologize for what happened, and she's come to see that I wasn't a terrible boyfriend, but a terrible boyfriend for *her*. We weren't compatible at all, and our relationship shouldn't have lasted near as long as it did. She also reassured me about the one line that stuck in my mind more than anything else..." He swallows. "The line about how I would make a horrible father. I...I always wanted kids, and that hurt a lot, and I believed it."

"Drew! You didn't tell me about that part. I don't remember it."

He shakes his head. "I was too ashamed. It was one of the reasons I broke up with you, because I suspected you wanted kids..." He looks at me questioningly.

I nod.

"...And I couldn't bear to give your kids a terrible father." He looks pained as he says the words. "But even if she hadn't reassured me about that, I wouldn't believe it anymore. I know I'm not terrible with children, and I don't need to be controlled by a book about embracing your inner ice cream sandwich."

"No, you don't." I pause for more ice cream. "If you were thinking about kids—"

"I'm serious about you, Chloe. I want a future with you. I don't know exactly what the future will hold, but I want it to be with you."

I climb onto his lap. I need to touch him. We kiss again, the lights of the city in the distance, the noise of traffic below...and the remains of an epic ice cream sundae on the table beside us.

I swipe up some whipped cream on my finger and feed it to him. He puts a dollop of whipped cream on my collarbone and licks it off. I try to feed him a maraschino cherry, but he shakes his head. "I don't like them, but I figured you did."

"You're not going to change your mind about maraschino cherries, like you did with ice cream?"

"No, I don't think so."

That's okay. We don't have to like all of the same stuff.

But I'm glad he can now appreciate ice cream, since I do own an ice cream parlor.

"Which is your favorite?" I ask, gesturing to the bowl with my spoon.

"The Vietnamese coffee."

"Good choice, but they're all good choices, since *I* made them. I can't wait for you to try the other flavors."

"We may have to wait until next week." He puts down his spoon, hauls me into his arms, and carries me inside to the bedroom.

I like where his mind is going.

We strip each other naked, and I sigh with pleasure when the length of his naked body presses against mine. We kiss, more and more frantically with each passing second, and I undulate my hips, wanting so desperately to join with him.

Finally, he rolls on a condom and enters me. It's such an amazing feeling, to be together like this. It feels so right. We move in sync, and he presses kisses all over my breasts and my chest and my neck. Everywhere he can reach.

We finish at the same time, finding our peaks of pleasure as one.

Afterward, I lie on my stomach, my head turned toward Drew, who runs his hand up and down my back. I smile lazily at him.

This is the life.

I'm full of ice cream and blissed out on sex, and now I'm lying in bed naked with the person I love more than anything, while Havarti Sparkles keeps watch from the bedside table.

"Have you had any terrifying dreams about unicorns lately?" I ask.

"Not since last week."

"Baby steps." I glance around his bedroom. It looks just like it did before, except…

I bolt upright. "What's hanging on the back of your door? Did you actually buy a unicorn onesie?"

"Um, well…"

"Ooh, can we get matching ones?"

"No, we can't get *matching* unicorn onesies. You can buy your own if you want, but it can't be identical to mine. I have a mental block when it comes to wearing the same thing as the woman I'm dating. Seems a little lame."

"And yet you bought a unicorn suit."

"You said it would make you laugh, and that's the best sound in the world. Well, it's a tie between that and when you come." He presses a kiss to my lips. "I have a small gift for you." He reaches into his bedside table and pulls out something colorful.

It's an ice cream cone amigurumi.

"It's so cute!" I exclaim. "I love it."

"I'm glad."

"But I'm not going to sleep until you try on that unicorn onesie for me."

"Just so you know, I will only wear it once a month, no more than that. There are limits to what my dignity will withstand."

"For a whole day once a month?" I bounce on the bed. "Twenty-four hours?"

He scowls at me as he gets up and pulls on his boxers, then puts on the unicorn onesie. When he starts to zip it up, I shake my head.

"Leave it undone so I can see your chest," I say.

He pushes up the hood so the mane, ears, and unicorn horn are visible. As is his scowl. "Are we done?"

I climb out of bed and wrap an arm around him, sliding my other hand up his bare chest.

"No," I whisper. "We're just getting started."

That night, I fall asleep in Drew's arms, with a unicorn onesie thrown over the chair next to the bed and my heart full of love and hope.

This is where I belong.

It's MID-SEPTEMBER, and the busy season at Ginger Scoops is winding down. After Thanksgiving in October, we'll only be open four days a week, Thursday through Sunday. I'm excited to have more time off, and we'll close for a few weeks at some point so I can take a much-needed vacation.

Today, however, the weather is still warm, and I'm glad. It's Saturday, and before opening at noon, I have both my family and Drew's family over to Ginger Scoops so they can meet each other. Aunt Anita is in town with her family for the weekend, and my father, my grandmother, my grandmother's boyfriend, Lillian, and Lillian's husband are also here. Lillian is very pregnant and will give birth any day now. Drew's parents have come with Adrienne, Nathan, and Michelle.

It's going okay so far. Everyone has their own cup of ice cream, and a few people have elected to try my special flavor of the month: mooncake. My mother preferred mooncakes with red bean filling; my dad and I preferred lotus. The mooncake ice cream is red bean-flavored with small pieces of salted egg yolk. My grandmother is particularly fond of it, which no longer surprises me. Dad decided to forgo the mooncake ice cream in favor of ginger and passionfruit, but he tries a bite of mine.

"Your mother would have loved this," he says.

Yes, she would have, but unfortunately, I've had to build a life without her.

I glance at the photo on the wall and smile.

Dad and I are in a much better place now. He's no longer questioning all my life decisions, and I feel like I can talk to him, even if he doesn't always understand.

Having finished my mooncake and ginger ice cream, I set down my cup and rest my head on Drew's shoulder. He puts his arms around me, and even though I get to touch him every day—we live together now!—this never gets old. I love every touch, every word he whispers in my ear.

"Cousin Chloe!" Keisha runs up to me with a drawing in her hand. Keisha, Sasha, and Michelle have been drawing in the corner together since they finished their ice cream. "I drew a picture for you."

It's a man and a woman. The woman is wearing a dress, and I think that's a veil? There are streamers with bells hanging overhead.

"It's you and Drew getting married," she says.

"It's lovely," I say. "When will our wedding be?"

"Next spring!"

"I don't know if it'll be that soon. But…one day."

"You should have a big wedding, like Meghan Markle and Prince Harry."

"Um. I doubt it will be quite that big, but I'll keep it in mind."

Michelle rushes over to Drew. "This is for you. It's a picture of you riding a unicorn and eating an ice cream cone!"

"Thank you. It looks just like me."

She giggles.

"I hear you're talking about weddings," Drew's mom sits down across from me.

"Well…"

"I already made the guest list."

"Mom!" Drew says. "I haven't even proposed."

"Maybe you should work on that. At least this one won't leave you at the altar."

I'm glad to have Drew's family in my life. His mom seems to have gotten over her disappointment that I'm not a doctor or an engineer and didn't finish university. She keeps telling her friends to come to Ginger Scoops.

The ice cream shop is doing reasonably well, and I'm happy with how the first summer went. There were even a few Saturdays when the line-up went out the door. The problem with my job, however, is that I don't have the weekends free to spend with Drew, but we spend every night together now that I've moved in with him.

I look around my shop, with its pink walls and rocking unicorn and cute stuffed alpacas on the shelf.

Most importantly, though, Ginger Scoops is currently full of family, of people who are important to me and Drew. Our fathers are talking about golf, Lillian and Deidre are talking about pregnancy, Grandma is explaining her recipe for lime Jell-O salad to Adrienne, Sasha is showing Anita the picture she drew of a T-Rex who can't eat ice cream because his arms are too short.

And the man I love presses a chaste kiss to my cheek and promises to do more—much more—after I finish work.

When I get home from Ginger Scoops at ten o'clock that night, Drew is sitting in the recliner, a bottle of bourbon barrel-aged imperial stout and a bar of chocolate beside him. There's a half-finished elephant amigurumi in his lap.

Yes, my boyfriend now crochets.

It took him a little while to get good at it, and the first thing he made was basically a deformed worm, but he's since crocheted me a pretty decent snail and an octopus. Now he's working on a butterfly.

"How was your day?" he asks, setting aside his crocheting.

"Good." I collapse onto his lap.

"Are you too tired to take me up on my promise?"

"Ha! No. But let's just stay here for a few minutes first." I wrap my arms around his neck. "I was talking to Anita about going to China one day. Flying into Hong Kong and visiting Guangzhou, then my family's ancestral village. Maybe you and I could do that together?"

"Of course." He presses a kiss to my temple, and I burrow against him.

I know that in China, I'll feel like I don't fit in. As I do in Chinatown, and when I walk into a room where everyone is white.

That's okay. I'm glad to be who I am, and I've found my place in the world. Ginger Scoops might be a cheery ice cream shop, but it provides me with the connection to my mom that I craved, and it makes me happy. I wouldn't call those things "frivolous".

Ginger Scoops also led me to Drew.

When I first met Drew Lum and he ordered a single black coffee rather than ice cream, I never imagined that one day, I'd be overwhelmed with love for him.

How things have changed.

I start unbuttoning his shirt as I kiss his lips, sighing in contentment when I get my hands on his bare chest. I'm so incredibly lucky to come home to him every day. He definitely doesn't melt my inner ice cream sandwich, even if that's what most of the world thinks.

No, he's the man who cherishes me for who I am, the man who makes me feel like I can accomplish anything. A man who will make a great husband and father one day.

We're going to have an amazing life together. I know it.

"Take me to bed," I whisper.

And he does just that.

ACKNOWLEDGMENTS

Thank you to my editor, Latoya C. Smith, for helping me make this book the best it could be, as well as Alana Delacroix, Chelsea Outlaw, and angel G for their assistance with the manuscript. The wonderful cover was created by Flirtation Designs.

Thank you also to Toronto Romance Writers, plus my husband and father, for all your support.

ABOUT THE AUTHOR

Jackie Lau decided she wanted to be a writer when she was in grade two, sometime between writing "The Heart That Got Lost" and "The Land of Shapes." She later studied engineering and worked as a geophysicist before turning to writing romance novels. Jackie lives in Toronto with her husband, and despite living in Canada her whole life, she hates winter. When she's not writing, she enjoys gelato, gourmet donuts, cooking, hiking, and reading on the balcony when it's raining.

To learn more and sign up for her newsletter, visit jackielaubooks.com.

ALSO BY JACKIE LAU

Kwan Sisters Series

Grumpy Fake Boyfriend

Mr. Hotshot CEO

Chin-Williams Series

Not Another Family Wedding

He's Not My Boyfriend

Baldwin Village Series

One Bed for Christmas (prequel novella)

The Ultimate Pi Day Party

Ice Cream Lover

Man vs. Durian

CPSIA information can be obtained
at www.ICGtesting.com
Printed in the USA
FFHW021826080719
53466844-59134FF